FLIGHT FROM MONTEGO BAY

FLIGHT FROM MONTEGO BAY

Alec Haig

A RED BADGE NOVEL OF SUSPENSE

DODD, MEAD & COMPANY
NEW YORK

ISBN: 0-396-06714-X
Library of Congress Catalog Card Number: 72-6880
Printed in the United States of America
by The Haddon Craftsmen, Inc., Scranton, Penna.

To Nancy

UNFINISHED BUSINESS

The Delta began its descent into Rome. Micky, the only stewardess in first class, crossed herself as she always did when they started landing, even though she had flown hundreds of hours. Da Vinci in ten minutes, Old Rome in half an hour and then, if nothing better offered itself meanwhile, a spaghetti supper with Don in his crazy apartment six floors above the street where they still manufacture antiques.

The bulkhead door opened and Skipper Bates came through. A captain-under-training was at the helm and Skipper Bates always made a point of leaving the flight deck for a few moments to let his trainees taste the acid fear of responsibility. He'd be back in his seat for the last crucial minutes of touch-down.

Micky handed the skipper his usual pre-landing cup of coffee, black without sugar the way he liked it. She offered one to the sole passenger in first class, but he declined with a smile and a shake of his head. The skipper drained his cup in one gulp then said to the passenger, 'We'll be touching down in five minutes, Mr Haig. I was wondering . . . Would you like to take her down, or shall I?'

Alec Haig smiled again. 'You take her down, skipper. I want to tell your stewardess where I'm taking her for supper tonight.'

The car that met Alec Haig at da Vinci airport stopped outside a solid old house overlooking the Tiber near Castel Sant' Angelo. When he rang the bell of the penthouse apartment, the door opened in a flurry of welcome from Aida, who had obviously seen the car arrive.

Aida was fifty, had few grey hairs, and a warm welcoming smile. The apartment was old, the doors thick and made of carved wood blackened with age. The furniture was old, solid, and comfortable. The terrace was covered in flowering shrubs, pots, trailing vines, creeping roses.

'I see you like the simple life,' Micky said. Alec burst out laughing, then led her up a winding spiral staircase. On the roof was another terrace, at least fifty feet square, also entwined with flowers and trailing plants. One half of the terrace was roofed with glass and contained a hammock sofa covered in towelling material that looked soft as swansdown. In the centre of the terrace was a swimming pool, half under the glass roof. The water was clear, blue, and totally inviting. Alec walked behind the hammock and when he came out again, naked, he flashed across the few feet of the terrace and dived into the water without a ripple.

'What the hell . . .?' Micky said out loud, then she grinned, unbuttoned her hostess uniform, and stepped out of it. When Alec rose to the surface at her feet, she stood poised at the pool's edge above him, then jack-knifed impeccably over his head and into the water. He smiled to himself. Only a whore would have insisted on wearing a swimsuit.

✳   ✳   ✳

Alec Haig rubbed the side of Micky's nose, gently coaxing her from sleep. She smiled without opening her eyes. He turned on to his side, touching all the way along her luscious body. He wiped his finger along her lower lip, slowly caressing her back to full consciousness. She opened her mouth slightly, and nibbled his finger. She turned to him, but he drew gently away from her. 'We have to get up,' he said.

He climbed out of bed. She opened her eyes.

'Would Skipper Bates really have let you land his plane?' she asked.

Alec nodded. He went through to the bathroom, showered and shaved. When he came out again, Micky was looking at several large parcels the Italian had brought into the bedroom.

'They've got my name on them,' Micky said. 'Who knew I was here?'

'I did,' Alec Haig said, and kissed her on the mouth. The Italian opened the parcels and spread their contents on the bed. Micky gave a moue of disappointment. 'I wanted to open them myself,' she said. But her eyes opened wide and sparkled when she looked at the garments, panties and brassiere in gossamer-thin silk, tights so fine they were almost invisible, a leather shirt soft as cashmere and twice as thin, a classic simple leather skirt with two large patch pockets, and a pair of leather ankle boots. And all in the most brilliant peacock blue, warmer in shade than any blue she'd ever seen, rich as the Mediterranean sea.

'And what's more,' she said, 'I bet it all fits perfectly . . .'

It did, of course.

To cap Micky's outfit, Alec Haig had provided a blonde wig, set in Grecian curls and ringlets.

When she put it on with the rest of the outfit, she looked and felt like a million dollars.

Alec and Micky arrived together at the Footwear Fashion Show in Alec's converted Lamborghini Special. Cameras clicked as Micky got out of the car, and adam's apples gulped for air. She was a knock-out, even among some of the most professional competition in the world. There were gasps and envious looks as together they walked down the corridor which led to a high vaulted chamber a hundred yards long and fifty yards wide, along the sides of which the shoemaker's stands had been arranged.

A knot of journalists gathered around Alec Haig and Micky, eyeing her costume appreciatively. The woman from *Elle* magazine examined Micky's outfit in great detail, then turned smiling to Alec. 'You don't catch us out like that, Mr Haig. This girl isn't one of your professional models . . .'

'Thank you at least for that,' Micky said, self composed beneath the scrutiny.

A little man, Carlo Vestispucci, sidled up to Alec Haig. He had the smile of a grubby schoolboy who's just put itching powder in a girl's knickers . . . 'Good morning, Mr Haig,' he said, bowed low to Micky, and smirked. 'That's a most elegant outfit you're wearing, Miss.'

'I'm pleased you like it . . .'

'But I fear you are in for a shock. Alec ought to have warned you, the bad man . . .'

And then the exhibition was opened by a fanfare of trumpets, and the curtains on all the stands were drawn wide, as if by the same cord.

Carlo Vestispucci gave a strangled howl as his eye ran down the hall. The shoes on the stands, the ankle-length boots, the curtains elegantly draped, the clothing of the stunning models were all in the same peacock blue Micky was wearing. All, all, blue. Save one. His own stand. Fifty thousand dollars he'd paid for that machine to print the

4

leather to the pattern he'd been told would be the sensation of the year, an imitation crocodile in nugget brown on mustard yellow. And he'd made thigh boots, and sling-back wedge heels—and dammit and curse Santa Maria of the Thieves of Bologna, there wasn't another print in the exhibition, not another thigh boot, not another wedge heel, not another sling-back shoe.

'You bastard,' Carlo said, 'you double-crossing bastard.'

Alec put his arm through Carlo's, and whispered. 'Industrial espionage is a game for professionals,' he said. 'When you started stealing our secrets, I knew within a few days. We've been feeding you with wrong information for months.'

Carlo Vestispucci was going to have either a fit or a coronary attack. Alec manœuvred him into a nearby chair, sat him down compassionately, then bent over him.

'When the market opened in London this morning, we dumped a block of your shares. Of course, *we* got a good price since we were first, but I reckon that by midday the quotation will hit rock bottom. I hope your liquidity is all right, Carlo, because you're going to need to pump a lot of ready money into that company to keep it afloat, especially when the banks learn you won't earn a penny this year from the rubbish you've been making . . .'

He straightened up. Carlo looked at him. 'You bastard, you've ruined me,' he said.

Alec looked down on him, ice flashing in his eyes.

'I hope so. If I have my way, you'll never make a foot of leather again, nor a single pair of shoes, and when the liquidators have finished with your company, you'll be living off spaghetti for the rest of your life.'

Alec grasped Micky's arm. 'Let's go to Doney's for an ice-cream,' he said, 'I could use the fresh air.'

5

INSTECON

INTERNAL MEMORANDUM Distribution A only
FROM: Head of Accounts
TO: Head of Tech. Sales (Misc.)

I refer to your last expenses vouchers and in
particular Item 4 on page 14 (purchase of
one locket/pendant/watch). Since this is an
item of capital expenditure, I would be
grateful if you would observe correct
procedure and deliver the same to Head of
Stores, for inclusion into his Stock Report.

Failing this, I regret I must deduct ninety
Swiss Francs, being the purchase price of the
said item, from the total of your expense
vouchers.

Alternatively, should the item be no longer
available for stock inclusion, please let me
have in triplicate a report giving the exact
circumstances in which the item was lost,
together with a Statement of Loss which, I
need not remind you, needs to be countersigned
by another director.

                signed J. C. Crump, Head of Accounts.

INSTECON

INTERNAL MEMORANDUM Distribution A only
FROM: Head of Tech. Sales (Misc.)
TO: Head of Accounts

My dear Crump,
I enclose the report you ask for. Let's hope
this time you'll read it. I'm sorry about the
locket/pendant/watch; however your aesthetic
sense will be pleased to know that, since it
was of vulgar and flashy design, it is no loss
to this company.
                        Alec Haig
                        Head of Tech. Sales (Misc.)

PHASE 1

They were sitting together in the corner of the drawing office when the nightwatchman came in, three men sipping coffee from the machine in the corner of the room, working late in the faithful service of a good employer. The dog with the nightwatchman growled. He touched the dog with the tip of his finger, and the dog was silent again, but watching.

'Aven't you gentlemen got no 'omes to go to?' he asked cheerfully, walking towards them, remembering training. His left hand dropped down, touching the dog's head again. One pressure and the dog would leap forward at them.

'Be about another hour, Fred,' Ben Thomas said.

'I 'ope you're on overtime . . .' Nearer now, near enough. Fingers on the dog's head. Stop. The dog stops, still. 'Don't often see you 'ere this late, Mr Lovell,' Fred said, looking at the second man of the trio.

Arthur Lovell grunted, in no mood for social chat with a nightwatchman.

Fred turned to the third man. Nice and easy, slow, relaxed. 'Don't think I've 'ad the pleasure of meeting you, sir?' Fred said. He lifted his fingers slightly in the dog's head. The dog growled, on cue. 'Quiet, Tiger,' Fred said. 'You'll 'ave to exuse my dog 'ere. 'E 'asn't 'ad the pleasure of meeting you either and 'e gets very upset wi' strangers.'

7

The third man, Samy Brunel, reached inside his pocket and drew out his company identification, and a pass. 'Funny thing, sir,' Fred said, 'I can see your pass was stamped and initialled at the door, but there's no sign of your name on the board, telling me you were still in the building.'

'You can't blame Mr Brunel if your section is slack,' Arthur Lovell grunted. 'Now if you don't mind . . .'

'Don't forget to lock everything away, will you, gentlemen, and give us a ring when you want letting out of the front door,' Fred said as he went out of the drawing office.

The three men watched him go. 'Damn,' Ben said, 'I forgot about entering your name on the blackboard . . .'

'Don't fret yourself,' Arthur said. 'They're all as thick as planks, anyway.'

Security was tight at the office of the Instecon Aircraft Company in Northamptonshire; each office contained a safe in which all documents must be locked overnight, each office door was sealed with a special lock that flashed a light in the guard house whenever it was opened, each building had its own security guard with a dog trained to sniff any intruder, and the whole complex of offices, hangars, engineering workshops and landing strips was enclosed in an electrified fence. Instecon's DELTA had arrived upon the aircraft world like a meteor, and airlines were fighting each other to buy it. The Delta had a cruising speed of a thousand miles per hour; it held a hundred people in absolute comfort but, most important, it had the lowest operating cost per passenger mile of any aircraft in the world. Its engines had been developed in great secrecy by Instecon Engineering; its airframe was developed, again without a whisper to the outside world, by Instecon Aeronautics. There wasn't a single aircraft designer or manufacturer in the world who wouldn't give his right arm to look at the drawings the three men had

projected from microfilm on the screen before them. Ben Thomas was a section leader, with an Instecon grade of B3 (engineering) and a salary of £4,500 per annum. Arthur Lovell was B5 (engineering), salary £2,500 per annum. A man of forty-two, he would have made the B3 grade long ago if he hadn't had a personality defect noted on his Instecon Personal Staff Data tape, which rated him 'hard to work with'. Arthur Lovell had a permanent chip on his shoulder, a grammar school boy who'd never learned to rise above his humble social origins, who thought that everyone who spoke the Queen's English with middle-class accents was necessarily an enemy. If his feelings had been political he would not have been allowed to work in such a sensitive section but he hated the communists almost as much as the liberals, lumped the socialists and the conservatives together as a bunch of thieving rogues. Arthur Lovell's objections to this life, had he but known it, stemmed almost entirely from feelings of social and sexual inadequacy.

The third man, Samy Brunel, was officially on an exchange visit from Instecon in Lille, France. His grade was B2 (administration) and his salary the equivalent of £5,500 per annum. Arthur Lovell automatically despised him.

Samy Brunel looked in a loose-leaf book that stood beside the microfilm projector. All the drawings relating to the Delta aircraft, some 270,000, were stored on microfilm in this cabinet, and any could be selected by punching the buttons on a panel.

'Let's look at 187736,' Samy Brunel said.

Arthur Lovell punched the appropriate set of buttons and the picture on the screen changed. This was a drawing of the oil feed system of part of the engine on the port side of the tailplane. They studied it for a few minutes, then Ben Thomas moved towards the screen, which measured five feet by four

9

and was filled with the lines and hieroglyphics of a conventional engineering drawing. 'This pipe,' Ben said, pointing to the centre of the drawing. 'If we were to put a by-pass inside the pipe, we could feed through this knuckle joint, round this bend, and divert the oil flow back into the main oil reservoir.'

'And all the time, the oil would show full pressure on the gauge,' Samy Brunel said.

'The vane would be starved of lubricant, and would overheat,' Ben added, his eyes bright with concealed excitement. Perhaps, at last, they had it . . .

'Yes,' Ben Thomas said, gripped by mounting excitement. 'but that wouldn't show because there's no temperature reading on that vane . . . You know, I think we've got it. You could make the by-pass in France and ship 'em over. You could say it was for the forward feeder. We could make a drawing-board mistake, impossible to trace, and the by-pass could be installed here instead of at the forward end where it should be . . .'

'It would take fifty flying hours before the vane would fracture, by which time all the planes could have been fitted . . .'

'And one by one,' Ben said, 'the whole bloody fleet would come tumbling out of the sky . . .'

'No such luck,' Samy said. 'They'd ground the fleet when the first one failed.'

Arthur Lovell had been watching the two other men with great disdain. 'I can't think what they pay you two buggers such exalted salaries for,' he sneered. He walked across to the screen. 'Look here,' he said, making no attempt to conceal his contempt, as if they were two schoolboys who thought they'd just disproved Pythagoras. 'If you starve the vane of oil, you also starve the linkage, don't you, since the linkage

10

gets its oil supply from the vane. If you starve the linkage, it also will overheat, and once it rises beyond a couple of hundred degrees, or whatever the thermocopile temperature is set at, the bi-metal strip will throw over, and bring in a fresh supply of oil from this pipe. Damn it, that's what we designed this supplementary supply for in the first place – or were you both asleep when we put that into the system . . .?'

'*Merde*, he's right,' Samy said.

'I know I'm right. And I also know I'm right when I keep telling you there's no way you can sabotage that plane without the maintenance engineers becoming aware of it. The plane's fool-proof. Your only hope is to get aboard one of 'em just before the take-off, when the maintenance engineers have given it the all clear, and do your damage then. But, of course, you won't listen to me, I'm only a B5.' He put his hands in his pockets and turned to face them.

'Why do you think Instecon insists on having a Chief Engineer do the pre-flight check?' Ben said. 'To prevent that very thing. You know as well as I do that the last man off a Delta before it's handed over to the airline is an Instecon staff man, minimum grade, B2.'

'Then that's the target. Buy a staff man . . .'

'Impossible,' Samy said.

'Why?' Arthur Lovell asked mulishly. 'They bought the three of us, didn't they? And you're B2.'

'Because the Chief Engineers who do the pre-flight check are all Alec Haig men, that's why. He picks 'em and makes damn sure they're loyal to him. He pays 'em extra as security men, and they are beyond temptation . . .'

'I still insist they are the target,' Arthur said. 'Get at a Chief Engineer doing his pre-flight test, and we can rig a plane to fall out of the sky any time we like . . .'

'How . . .'

11

'By reversing the bi-metal strip. Get out the drawings, and I'll show you . . .'

*   *   *

'How many in first class?' Micky asked the purser, as she went aboard the New York flight.

'Only one,' he said. 'Must be a VIP. He's reserved the whole cabin to himself.'

Micky was standing inside the cabin lobby when he came aboard. 'Good evening,' she said, her official sing-song voice well regulated, all feeling, all personal emotion erased. 'Welcome aboard our flight to New York. My name is Micky, and I shall be at your disposal during this flight, so don't hesitate to ask me for anything you may require . . .'

'If you mean that,' Alec Haig said, as he seated himself in the leather-upholstered armchair, 'this plane travels much too quickly.'

She walked up the aisle and stood beside his chair. 'Why did you pick this flight?' she asked. 'I thought we'd said goodbye once.'

'Business,' he said. 'I have to get to New York as soon as possible. I'm sorry. I thought we'd said goodbye, too.'

'One thing I'll say about you,' Micky said. 'You don't mess about. You don't cheat, like so many men do. You don't go in for the "for ever and ever" bit. I like that. With you, everything's honest and straightforward. Like toast, crisp when it's hot, lousy and soggy once it's cold. I like that.'

She bent down and quickly kissed his forehead.

*   *   *

The Instecon Building in New York is on Sixth Avenue, south of the Time-Life Building. It stands thirty-three storeys high, but is only the American branch office. The main building is on the lake side at Zürich, in Switzerland. The company helicopter was waiting for Alec at Kennedy Airport when the Delta arrived, on time as usual. The company expeditor, Sol Lefkowitz, had already cleared Alec through Customs and Immigration, and he was able to walk straight across the tarmac and on to the helicopter which whisked him in minutes to the top of the Instecon Building in Manhattan. He entered a small lobby on the roof, opened the waiting lift door, and pressed his thumb against a frosted-glass plate, ignoring the row of buttons marked with each of thirty floors. The magic eye read his thumb-print, closed the door, and the lift descended.

The top three floors of the building were isolated from the other floors, and access to them could only be gained by thumb-print selection. Alec's print took him to the top floor but one.

He came out of the lift, turned right, and walked along a carpeted corridor to a door at the far end, on which a plate read 'Technical Sales, (Misc)'. Ken was waiting in the office.

'Sol called, said you were on your way. How've you been? Had a good flight? Need a drink or anything?'

'Thank you, Ken, I've just been fine. The flight was fine. I don't need a thing. How have you been?'

'Just fine. Madonna has messages . . .'

'Madonna has messages like a teen-ager has acne!' Alec crossed the outer office and the door to the inner office opened before he touched it. Madonna had her foot on the switch. She was sitting at her desk, looking at her steno pad, wearing her thick spectacles. She was a woman about fifty, fat, dumpy, with soft blonde hair on her upper lip, but could take steno in three languages faster than Alec could speak them, type at competition speed, and never forgot a date nor a fact.

'What kept you?' she asked in mock severity. 'That goddam plane's been on the ground for fifteen minutes.'

He unbuttoned the collar of his white silk shirt, pulled his tie down a notch, and sat in the leather armchair next to her desk. She filled a cut crystal glass from the water cooler, handed it to him without a word, and opened her pad again. 'Whaddya want, the whole bag of tricks, or an expurgated version . . . ?'

'I'll have the lot. Get it over and done with.'

'Johnny called from Texas and he wants a programme for the launch. I've prepared a folder with the Cape Kennedy details, and Ken's updated it.'

'Send it.'

'Friedman called from Boston. He's plugged that leather leak; some guy was making handbags at home . . .'

'Fifty thousand feet a month . . . ?'

'Yeah; all his relatives were working with him and they'd rented a loft.'

'Was he doing good business?'

'Making a fortune . . . Friedman wants to prosecute . . .'

'Tell O'Connell in accounts to look at the operation. If he likes it, we could stake the man and he could pay us back for his theft with shares . . .'

'Good thinking, Mr Haig . . . Al Kopotna called from LA. They found out who was bugging the phones.'

'Students?'

'That's right, Mr Haig, how did you know?'

'Intuition, smell, plus the fact that we make a part in that factory that's used in military planes.'

One by one she went through the messages, and he dealt

with each in turn. It took forty-five minutes. He went through to his own inner office, showered and changed into a lightweight, dark business suit. He was tying his plain blue-striped tie when she called him on the intercom.

'Mr Haig. They're going into the boardroom now.'

He spoke from where he was, knowing the microphone would pick up his voice easily.

'Very good, Madonna, I shall be at their disposal in two minutes.'

She sighed deeply. 'One of these days, Mr Haig, I'm gonna meet a guy in Brooklyn who talks just the way you do, with that accent an' all, and when I do, poweee . . .'

He chuckled. On the salary he paid her, she could afford to live in Sutton Place South . . . 'You're putting me on . . .' he said.

Alec Haig stood over six feet tall, weighed 185 pounds, and walked with the grace of a ballet dancer. But there the resemblance ended. During the last world war he had fought in North Africa with the Long Range Desert Group; he met Colonel Peniakoff in Cairo and was induced to join Popski's Private Army; when their hit-and-run raids ended with the rout of Rommel's 'invincible' army, he volunteered to fly gliders into Europe for the Second Front. In 1945 when he left the army he'd collected an MM and bar, an MC and bar, and five wounds, none of which he ever showed in public.

Once he had been married to a lovely girl; she was killed in an air crash flying to compete in the International Piano Festival in Yorkshire, England. From that moment, air safety became one of his chief passions. He personally had influenced the Instecon board to spare no costs when they devised the Delta to be the safest plane in the air; he insisted that he personally train the chief maintenance engineers who handed the planes over to the pilots; he screened them, and insisted they be paid sufficient to remove them from any industrial espionage or sabotage temptations. Among other benefits, the children of each of these engineers was educated at company cost at private schools; Alec knew that few men will hazard their kids' educations. He taught the men all the latest techniques of industrial sabotage, constantly harried the engineering boffins to devise ways in which the plane could be protected against intrusion. Example: if anyone attempted, either deliberately or accidentally, to put anything other than the correct fuel into the plane, a siren would wail. If anyone tampered with the operating linkage of the tail-plane, a light would come on in the console under the belly of the plane to which only the chief maintenance engineer had access. The Delta was a vandal-proof plane, as safe as a Rolls-Royce motor car, and Alec was proud of his share in that.

They were all sitting round the boardroom table when he arrived. At the head of the table Sir Barton Underwood, fourteenth baronet of a feudal line that went back to William the Conqueror. He smiled his somewhat cold smile when Alec came into the room. 'Sorry to call the meeting here in New York,' he apologized to Alec and to the table in general, 'but it seemed the most convenient place to get us all together.' New York, Zürich, London, Tokyo, it was all the same to the directors of Instecon, whose ramifications covered the entire globe and, through their Polish and American aerospace affiliates, outer space as far as the moon. Kenneth Severs, in direct line of succession, was sitting next to Sir Barton at his

16

married man, with kids. Why should the kids suffer because of a momentary aberration of their father's?

'Anything we can do for the widow?' Alec asked, his anger temporarily held in check.

'Not officially, I'm afraid,' Sir Barton said. 'Think of the bad effect on our other people, the ones who don't cross the line, if we reward the fellow's widow.'

Alec looked round the table. Kenneth Severs wouldn't help, of course; he had a puritan's approach to crime, criminals, and their dependants. 'Fear of what will happen to their wives and kids is the only thing that keeps a lot of men honest,' he said, in his thin, nasal, New England voice.

'I'll see she's all right,' Jacques de Blaie said. 'They've been nagging at me to export my distillation to England as brandy. Ten thousand bottles a year. She can be the agent for it; she'll earn two thousand a year for writing a few letters . . .'

Alec had known Jacques would help; he'd known too that the money would not come directly from Jacques's own pocket.

'Can we get down to the main purpose of the meeting?' Sir Barton asked. He too had known Jacques de Blaie would make a gesture to get the company off the hook. 'I'll ask Mr Severs to report.'

Kenneth Severs fiddled with his glasses before he spoke, his mind no doubt scanning every possible track, every inference of what he was about to say. 'I feel out on a limb at the moment,' he said. 'As you all know my world is concerned with facts and figures. Interpretations I leave to you. So let me give you a few facts and figures, for openers. Last week the Personal Life Assurance Company of Boston's pension fund sold five hundred thousand shares of Instecon International.'

'What price did they get?' Jacques asked.

'They started at 305, went down to 303.'

'But that's crazy,' Jacques said. 'They're quoted at 306.25 in London this morning, and when the exchange opens in Tokyo in a couple of hours they'll move, without a shadow of a doubt, to 307 . . .'

'I know that. But let me continue. Deutsche Allgemeine-stellenwerk of Düsseldorf sold three hundred thousand last week, and they let them go for an average of 302.5 . . .'

'They've gone out of their minds!' Jacques said.

'Of course, the shares were snapped up quickly but all in small lots under fifty thousand. I've checked the share transfers and, gentlemen, I have to tell you that during the past month four million shares of Instecon International have changed hands. And, what is significant, the shares have come out of the institutional large holdings, and gone into small investors' hands.'

'And the price hasn't been affected,' Alec said, 'though I need hardly say that it would take only one financial journalist to ask questions and send our price plummeting.'

'The shares were sold,' Kenneth Severs said, 'in small amounts through regular brokers so as not to make waves. But, gentlemen, *il faut comprendre*,' he said, switching to French which they all spoke as fluently as English, Spanish, or German, 'Instecon International no longer has the confidence of the institutions.'

They were all silent for a moment, thinking. Their company was being blackballed by the most exclusive club in the world. 'Someone is spreading a rumour,' Jacques de Blaie said.

'But what about?' Sir Barton asked. 'On all fronts we're doing extremely well. Textiles, engineering, leather and footwear, mining, steel – now that Alec stopped them pinching our phosphorus-free formula – aerospace, aviation. I would have thought our success with the Delta alone would have assured everyone of our long-term stability, and guaranteed our growth potential. That plane is so far ahead of anyone else . . .'

'It *is* very much in the public eye,' Alec said. 'If anything ever went wrong with it . . .'

'What *can* go wrong? The plane's well-nigh perfect. Our latest V-tol version has passed every test with – if I might coin a phrase – flying colours. It has already received its certificate of airworthiness, and the order book is full. And, what's more important, we've proved you don't need to mess about with military versions of aeroplanes to make them pay . . .'

'But, nevertheless, someone is spreading a rumour,' Jacques de Blaie said. 'And at the highest level, not on the floor of the stock exchange.'

'Whatever they're doing,' Kenneth Severs said, 'it's being done on an international scale. The withdrawal of capital by the institutions is world-wide. It only needs one more really big one . . .'

'Then we must act quickly,' Sir Barton said incisively. 'If *we* know about this, other people must know, too, and they will be watching to see what we do. So, first, we must put up some kind of a show. You all know my personal dislike of flim-flam, but we cannot be seen to do nothing. You, Jacques, must mount some sort of a public relations affair that will reveal the true state of our businesses. Obviously we don't care what you spend, provided what you do is discreet, simple, tasteful, and completely comprehensible both to the small investor and the brokers. Don't worry too much about the institutions; I've always believed they get their information in the same way a plant gets its nourishment, by osmosis through what, to the common herd, is an impermeable membrane of silence. You must emulate Hercules, turn the river of enlightened opinion through what appear to have become our Augean stables . . .'

They all smiled at Sir Barton's turn of phrase; how typical of him to encompass both plant biology and ancient mythology.

'Meanwhile, Alec, while all this flim-flam is going on, you must do the real work. You must trace the source of these scandalous and malicious rumours, so that we can decide what to do about them.' There were no instructions to Alec. Sir Barton didn't like what Alec did any more that he liked public relations flim-flam, as he called it.

'And you, Kenneth, must look at our paperwork. You must examine every document we have made public during the past few months, every balance sheet, every financial statement and the efficiency of your accounts. Knowing you, I don't imagine you'll find any grounds for correction, but look at them again through a suspicious eye.'

Kenneth coughed discreetly. 'If you'll pardon a mixed metaphor, Sir Barton, I can see by the gleam in *your* eye that you've got something up your sleeve . . .'

Sir Barton permitted himself one of his rare smiles. 'The Heir to the throne of England, Prince Charles, and his father, His Royal Highness the Duke of Edinburgh, Prince Philip, have both expressed, through the appropriate Palace quarters of course, an interest in the Delta airplane. In commoners' parlance, their Royal Highnesses are itching to get behind the controls . . . I propose we give them our new V-tol version to play with. Perhaps we might persuade them to land it in the forecourt of Buckingham Palace, just before the Changing of the Guard . . .'

'No doubt with the Queen herself, and Princess Anne, waving from a balcony to a hundred thousand tourists . . . ?' Jacques de Blaie asked, smiling.

'Something like that. Dignified, simple, but quite effective.'

PHASE 2

Alec started his work in New York. Not downtown on Wall Street, but in 44th Street, just off Fifth Avenue, in the Harvard Club. George Phillimore was waiting for him when he arrived, led him across the lobby and into the smoking-room. They sat at the corner table at the far side of the room, traditionally used by members when they want to get away from everyone else. George Phillimore asked Alec what he'd like to drink, wrote it on the pad provided for orders, and handed it to the waiter.

While they were waiting for their drinks, they discussed the weather, Britain's entry into the Common Market, the chance of soccer ever catching the interest of the Americans. The waiter returned in due course. To have hurried would have been undignified.

Finally they were alone together.

'What's on your mind, Alec?' George asked, coming straight to the point. George Phillimore had been chairman of Peters, Prestwich, Padget and Bell before he struck out on his own in 1969. Since then he'd built a successful brokerage business, handling special lines in special cases for special clients. A man with a successful five years of trading history, but perhaps a doubtful product, wanted to bring his company to the market. Maybe this year, maybe next. He employed George Phillimore to 'advise'. If George, after investigation of the company's affairs, didn't think the flotation would attract sufficient attention this year, he said so. A film star had shares in the company to which she was contracted to make films. She proposed to break her contract, but first, she wanted to sell her shareholding without anyone being the wiser. She went to George Phillimore. He'd move her out of MGM and into Fox, out of Fox and into United Artists, CBS, Westinghouse, whichever company seemed to suit her future requirements. Nobody ever knew what George Phillimore did, except those on the inside, those for whom he was doing it.

'What could you do with half a million shares of Instecon International?' Alec asked.

George whistled silently. 'You want to sell out . . .?'

'I didn't say that. I merely asked what could you do with them.'

'How many again?'

'Five hundred thousand . . .'

George's mind worked like an adding machine. Five hundred thousand shares at over 300 per share, £3.00, was a lot of money. 'My God, Alec, I knew you weren't on the breadline, but I didn't realize you were *that* loaded . . .'

The remark from anyone else might have sounded offensive, but Alec was used to George's bluntness. 'I keep a piggy bank,' he said, smiling as he sipped his drink.

'How much time do we have?'

'No time at all.'

'My God, Alec, you can't just throw half a million shares of Instecon International on the market like that. Not if you want to hold 300 with them.'

'I want more than that. 305 minimum . . .

'Then you don't want them dumped.'

'No, but I'd like to sell them in one block.'

'I see. One block, 305 minimum, but obviously anything

above that I can get, and no dumping. And I guess since you want me to handle it for you, it's a hush-hush job?'

'That's right . . .'

'One of these days, just one of these days, one of you bastards is going to come to me with a piece of legitimate business . . .'

'You wouldn't have left P, P, P, and B, George, if you liked legitimate business . . .'

George had a gleam in his eye. 'My commission's pegged, of course, but the expenses might be high. After all, I've got to find the right Institution for you, and most of them are already in big with Instecon.'

'Then you'll just have to find one who isn't, won't you. And I shan't quibble about expenses.'

George finished his drink. 'Time for lunch?' he asked, but Alec shook his head. 'Can a fella ask a question?' George said. 'You thinking of quitting Instecon? Maybe going out on your own? I have a few Internationals tucked away in my granny-bag. For my old age, you know. But if you're going to rock the boat . . .'

'Who said I'm rocking the boat?' Alec asked. 'Leave your shares where they are; they'll see you through to a ripe and well-provided-for old age.'

George thought for a moment.

'You know how to find out quickly what chances you have of selling your shares without dumping them?'

'I thought you were the best man for that . . .'

'I am the best *man*. But there's a woman. You haven't thought about that, have you? Carla Pontisemi . . .'

'In Rome?'

'She's in New York. Penthouse apartment on Beekman. She's said to be a great lay, Alec. The greatest. You could find out all you want to know, and in bed . . .'

'I'll stay with you, George . . .'

'What's the matter, Alec. Never knew you pass up a woman before . . . not going queer in your old age, are you?'

'Look, George. I have my work, and I have my friends. Okay, I'm not a monk. I go to bed with a woman sometimes. But, believe it or not, I don't screw around in the line of business. As Sir Barton would say, there are some things a gentleman just does not do . . .'

George gave him a horse laugh. 'That's for the birds, Alec, and you damned well know it.'

'Oddly enough, it happens to be true . . .'

PHASE 3

British Amalgamated Airlines flight number 500 leaves for New York daily, at midday. On the 27th September the flight, as usual, was fully booked. The plane had flown the New York to London leg the previous evening and the maintenance engineers had taken over, working all night and most of the morning to check every single part. About four o'clock in the morning, Ross Compton, the Instecon staff engineer attached to British Amalgamated Airlines, listening with his stethoscope probe to the servo mechanism on the left rudder trimmer, had heard the suspicious noise of a partly worn bearing. It had taken until eight o'clock to replace it. One of the thrust rollers had a hairline crack in it, and though it would have been good for another fifty thousand miles, Ross Compton sealed it in a plastic bag after photographing it, and sent it to the Instecon laboratory in Hertfordshire. If, as he supposed, the part was faulty, he knew Instecon would play merry hell with the manufacturer. At half past eight Ross Compton washed his hands and took Charlie Lamport across to terminal seven for a bite of breakfast. 'Another hour should see us finished,' he said. 'And then we can hand her over to BAA.'

Lamport was a nervous, fussy man, an engineer of the old school. He was five feet ten, weighed far too much for that height, and bit his fingernails, despite their usually being smeared with engine oil and grease.

They ordered eggs, bacon, sausage, toast and marmalade. Ross drank coffee, Charlie drank tea. There was no sugar on the table Charlie had chosen, and Ross got up and went to the counter to get a bowl.

While he was away from the table, Charlie took the small bottle of liquid they'd given him, and poured it into Ross's coffee. They'd said it was odourless and tasteless, but Charlie was still worried when Ross, having stirred sugar into his coffee, drank it down in one gulp. 'I needed that,' he said.

Ross looked out of the window, then back at Charlie.

'There's no need to be so worried,' he said. 'That new bearing's running perfectly. I listened to it for five minutes. It's seated itself beautifully. Really, Charlie, you did a good job there. If it hadn't been for you, we'd still have been messing about, trying to get the bearing back in. I don't like to ground a Delta for mechanical failure, but I'd have grounded that one if the bearing hadn't gone in right, believe me. Like I said, you worry too much . . .'

They finished their breakfast in silence. Ross signed the bill, and they went together back across the apron to where the Delta was waiting. Together they entered the aircraft, and sat at the controls. 'Okay, Charlie,' Ross said, 'let's run 'em up.' Routine engine check . . . check all the procedures the pilot himself would check before the plane took off with its full load of passengers. Being engineers, however, the checks they carried out were regulated with mathematical precision. One, two, three, four, each engine fired and was run to maximum revs and each time the points were noted on the pad Ross had brought into the cockpit of the plane. One by one, each item on the long list was ticked off when the meter readings had been verified for oil pressure, electric charge positive/negative, temperature, air flow, and oil flow.

One by one the list of ticks grew longer as Ross turned the first page and then the second.

Finally he came to the last page. All appeared to have gone smoothly but Ross had not permitted himself to become complacent. How could he, anyway, with Charlie sitting beside him nervous as an old maid school-teacher checking that a pupil is working correctly? There had been no snags that Ross was aware of, nothing to justify Charlie's apparent unease.

'Take it easy,' Ross said, watching Charlie start on yet another fingernail, already down to the quick. He finished the last check, sat back and stretched to ease the tension of staring at the instrument panel and the cathode ray oscillo- scope that simulated flight conditions. Then his eye caught the panel clock and he swore as he verified it against his wrist- watch. 'By God, is that the time?' he asked, wiping his fore- head with his handkerchief.

They left the plane together. Ross checked the black box in its shock-proof mounting in the fuselage, the device that would tell the whole mechanical story in the extremely unlikely event the plane should crash. He set the box to 'record', then locked the cover. Even before the first engine was switched on, the box would start printing all the details of the plane's progress, a fifteen-track tape signal with ears and eyes fixed to each vulnerable part of the plane's fuselage and equipment. It would only cease recording after the last engine switched off, hopefully on the other side of the Atlantic. The Instecon security guard was standing by the tailplane, his dog alert beside him. 'It's all yours,' Ross said, and the guard nodded. No one would get near that plane until it was taken over by the airline staff, ready to fly.

Ross and Charlie went together to the Chief Engineer's

office, and Ross handed over the carbon copies of his check list, retaining the original for filing in his own office.

'Going home to bed now, Charlie?' he asked.

Charlie grunted. Ross felt a sudden surge of sympathy for him. Both Charlie's mother and father were crippled with arthritis. His mother had incurable diabetes and his father inoperable cancer. No hospital would accept them in its geriatric wards, since both were terminal cases who needed constant attention. Charlie did the best he could, but he had young kids at school, and a wife who couldn't get on with the nurses he was able to afford from time to time. God, what a mess, Ross thought. No wonder Charlie bites his nails. Luckily he seemed a man who didn't need much sleep. During the long hours of the nights they'd talked about Charlie's problems, but no solution offered itself. Charlie would look after both his parents when he got home, snatch a few hours' sleep during the afternoon, then tend his parents again before coming in to work. Usually he could leave the airport about seven o'clock, but if anything happened like last night, with that thrust bearing, then it would be eight, nine, ten, before Charlie could get away.

Ross said goodbye to Charlie at the employees' car park entrance, then turned and walked, forcing himself not to hurry, across the asphalt square to the Instecon Office, a two-storey building only recently completed. Though outwardly constructed of concrete and brick in the current airport style, the whole shell was encased in steel plates. The glass in the windows was shatter-proof and one-directional, the doors locked with tamper-proof systems, since no lock can be truly burglar-proof provided the would-be thief has time. Lights set on poles at each corner of the building made certain no one could have time to work unobserved on the outside of what was in effect a steel-and-concrete bunker.

30

With billions at stake, and several Delta aircraft a day flying into and out of London, Instecon was taking no chances.

Ross Compton opened the outer door, went into the small lobby. The time was ten o'clock. Elsie, the receptionist/telephone-operator was sitting behind the functional desk in the corner. Behind her was the board carrying the names of the engineers. All were marked 'out'. When Elsie saw Mr Compton arrive, she turned and flicked his indicator to the 'in' position. How he managed to cross the reception area Ross never knew. The sweat was now pouring from his forehead, and he could feel it running down his sides and between his legs. His own office was upstairs; he climbed the flight with difficulty. 'Are you all right, Mr Compton?' Elsie called after him, but he waved his arm limply at her and carried on. His office was at the head of the stairs, through his secretary's office. Mary Spengler was typing a report. When she saw the state he was in, the goodmorning greeting froze on her lips. She started to get out of her chair, but Ross waved her back again.

'I'm all right,' he said. 'Just a bit hot.'

He went through her office. Inside his own, he dared not sit down. He could feel his heart hammering, his skin burning as if he were in a Sauna bath, though the sweat on his body was cold and clammy, and he smelled sour. Three telephones on his desk. One internal to the building. One on to the normal exchange through Mary and the switchboard manned by Elsie. The other, a radio telephone, carried a built-in scrambler mechanism. In the corner was a radio with which he could talk to any Instecon engineer, anywhere in the airport, through the walkie-talkie sets all the engineers and guards carried. The radio was paralleled into the radio-room below, manned day and night throughout the year. By the radio was a tape recorder. He staggered across the room and switched it to position three, then started it. Anything said on his scrambler phone would now be recorded.

He took out a handkerchief and wiped his face. The handkerchief was immediately soaked. He put it down on the corner of his desk, took a hand towel from the cubicle which contained a wash basin, and wiped himself with that. Still the sweat poured. Vision perfect, breathing better, heart no longer pounding. He held out his hand. It was rock steady, his mind was clear, his reflexes good. But his memory had a damned great hole in it. He couldn't remember any of the details of the centre portion of the check he had just carried out on that plane. He could remember starting, remember the whole of pages one and two. He could remember the check finishing, again the whole of pages ten and eleven. But, Jesus Christ, what had happened to the pages between? He could remember Charlie sitting next to him, biting his fingernails, nervous as ever, looking at everything, checking and re-checking everything. Think, man, think. Let your mind run over the dials in that cockpit, the cathode ray oscilloscope. Think man. Remember the dial readings. Page three, he knew it by heart, but why couldn't he remember reading it during the check?

And Charlie, sitting there, beside him, biting his fingernails, nervous.

He looked at the pad. Pages one and two, all ticked. He turned the pad to page three, expecting to find it blank. But every tick was in position, in the black Pelican ink he always used in his fountain pen. A neat row of ticks, all the way down the page. Page four the same, and all the pages, the same. But why didn't he remember them? Page six. He should have remembered that. Especially since they'd changed the thrust bearing. A group of five ticks on page six would reconfirm that the thrust bearing had gone in all right, had bedded neatly, efficiently. He should remember that. Dammit, they'd just changed the bearing, hadn't they? And he could remember every single detail of the work they'd done, he and Charlie, and Moss and Sammy, working together through the night, and when Moss and Sammy had gone off shift, he and Charlie, working together, alone together, finally seating the roller bearing. But he couldn't remember any single one of the five checks that would have reassured them the bearing was all right. Charlie must have been content, or he wouldn't have let Ross make that tick, would he?

Ross picked up the scrambler telephone and dialled a number. He heard the signal as the number rang once at the other end, and the girl answered immediately. 'Four, zero,' she said.

'115.A1.4,' he replied. The girl understood him at once. *This is the Chief Engineer of Instecon at BAA Heathrow (115). and I want an Absolute Priority (A1) call to Mr Alec Haig (4).* Then he put the telephone back on to its cradle. Still the sweat was pouring down his forehead. Alec Haig could be anywhere in the world, but they'd find him quickly and get him to a telephone. But would it be quickly enough? He picked up the telephone again, dialled the same number, got the same four zero. '115.A1.33,' he said.

(33) meant, *I need a doctor.*

'Where?'

'My office. A1.'

'I got that the first time,' she said. 'Which do you want first? I now have 4 on the line for you.'

'I'll speak to 4, and you can arrange 33 meanwhile. And A1, lovey . . .'

'I got that the first time,' she repeated. Then her voice softened. 'Don't worry. I'll be as quick as I can.'

There was a click and Ross heard the voice he knew so well,

of Alec Haig. 'If we don't complete this call,' Ross said, '99.7.500.07/08/11.'

'Right,' Alec said. *If we don't complete this call, ground the BAA flight 500 to New York, and look for incomplete maintenance, (07) legitimate mechanical failure (08) or sabotage (11).*

'Okay,' Alec said, 'is there anything you need?'

'I've put out a 33.'

'Good man. What's the story?'

'I don't know ... You'll think I'm going crazy. I did a pre-flight check this morning ...'

'BAA 500 ...?'

'Yes. It took half an hour longer than it usually does. We changed a bearing during the night, and by the way, that's part number AB7/144439/70001 ...'

'I've got it ... Why did the pre-flight take so long?'

'That's what's worrying me. It was an absolutely normal check. The bearing had gone in well, and I'd checked everything there, and Charlie had checked everything ... but here's something else. I don't remember anything at all after page two of the check, until page ten. I've got a complete gap in my memory ...'

'What was the oil pressure on the starboard link connector ...'

'That's what I'm talking about. Dammit, from memory I can tell you that reading is slap in the middle of page four ...'

'It's also one of the most important readings, Ross, surely you appreciate that ...'

'I do. I do. But, I can't remember what it was ... My mind's a blank. It's ticked on the check list, so I must have read it, and the reading must have been okay, but *I can't remember what it was!*'

'Anything else? So far we know the check took an extra

half hour, and you can't remember many of the details, though you've ticked them on your check list . . .'

'Yes, one more thing. I'm sweating. Like a pig. And I keep in such good shape I never sweat. Two games of squash and I'm dry . . . but at this moment, I'm sweating like a pig . . .'

'Had any food today?'

'Breakfast in building Number 7.'

'Who with?'

'Charlie Lamport, of BAA.'

'Drink anything?'

'Only coffee . . .'

'Leave the table . . .?'

Ross thought, but it was an effort. Now the sweat was pouring down his face. 'Yes, come to think of it. I went to get the sugar bowl.'

'Anybody else at the table? Or just Charlie Lamport.'

'That's right. Just the two of us.'

'Where is he now?'

'Gone home . . .'

'Mother and father still living with him.'

'You have a good memory, Mr Haig . . .'

'Still both ill? What was it, diabetes and cancer?'

'And arthritis. Charlie nurses 'em, since he can't afford anybody full time and they could last for a year or two . . .'

'Take your pulse rate; better still, call it out to me.'

Ross put a finger on his pulse and called the beats over the telephone.

'Okay,' Alec said, 'you can stop now.'

There was a sudden knock on the door. Mary Spengler stood there, and behind her a young man wearing spectacles and carrying the traditional black bag. 'A man here, Mr Compton, says you've sent for him?'

'Let him in,' Ross said.

The man came through the doorway, put his bag on the desk.

'It's 33,' Ross said into the telephone.

'Ask him to look at you. I'll hold on,' Alec said.

The young doctor had a smooth deskside manner. 'Now what seems to be the trouble?' he asked.

Ross felt like screaming at him, but restrained himself. 'I think I've been given something.'

Already the doctor was standing immediately in front of Ross, and lifted one of his eyelids. He'd taken a small torch from his black bag and shone it directly into Ross's eye.

'What do you think it was? A drug, or a poison . . .?'

'What's the difference . . .'

'With drugs you pass out . . . with poison you peg out . . .'

'Cheerful bugger . . .'

'Open your mouth . . .'

'I haven't cleaned my teeth this morning yet . . .'

'That's the least of our problems. In a while we may be pumping out your stomach and emptying your bladder and your bowels . . .'

The doctor examined Ross quickly, checked his pulse rate, blood pressure, heart beat, skin temperature. Then he told him to lie on the office sofa and went across to the telephone.

'Is that Mr Haig? This is Doctor Gervis.'

'Good afternoon, doctor.'

'It's morning here . . .'

'Yes, of course. What can you tell me about Mr Compton?'

'He thinks he's been drugged. Or poisoned. I can find no traces of anything wrong at the moment. Everything seems quite normal, heart, pulse, temperature. He's sweating pro-fusely, but that could just be fear. If he *thinks* he's been poisoned . . .'

'What do you suggest?'

'There's a nursing home not far from here. I use it quite a lot. It has a small laboratory attached, and I could take him apart there. I'd also like to call in a couple of consultants . . .'

'Is the laboratory secure . . .?'

'Guaranteed . . .'

'And you could get him there without his condition deteriorating . . .?'

'I think he's fit to move. Well, let me put it this way; I can find no reason why he shouldn't be moved . . .'

'Would you mind putting him on the telephone. And thank you for turning out so promptly . . .'

'I happened to be at the airport. It's my day for air-crew medical spot checks . . .'

The doctor carried the telephone on its long cord across to the sofa on which Ross Compton was half sitting, half lying, his face streaming with perspiration, his forehead dripping. He'd heard what the doctor had said. Nothing appeared to be wrong. But he was sweating. The doctor looked at him as he took the telephone in his hand. Was it only fear? Many things can make a man sweat.

Ross Compton raised the telephone to his ear and spoke softly into it. 'Ross Compton, Mr Haig . . .'

At that moment he died and the telephone slipped from his hand and clattered against his shoe as it dropped to the carpet.

PHASE 4

Alec Haig was in Hong Kong when he received the telephone call from Ross Compton. He had just asked Kwam T'ang to get him a price for half a million shares of Instecon International. He knew Kwam T'ang would consult the underground market, and the quotation would come from Switzerland. Kwam T'ang, with Oriental wisdom and inscrutability, recognized that he would never see the half million shares and that the words of the ancient philosopher Lin Po applied to this case – *The stars twinkle more brightly when the sun has hidden her face.* Kwam T'ang had charged a 'consultation' fee of one thousand American dollars, paid in cash. Both he and Alec Haig knew he'd get the equivalent of *five* thousand dollars on the Saigon black currency market, so he was quite happy to play the charade of selling the shares, looking for the information for which he knew Alec Haig would pay a further thousand dollars, in American cash. Kwam T'ang had just left Alec's office at Instecon (Far East), his face gleaming with pleasurable anticipation, protesting his undying loyalty and faithfulness, when the call came through from Heathrow. Alec acted immediately, and the Instecon Executive Delta took off from Hong Kong two hours after he put down the radio telephone on which he had talked via the satellite to Ross Compton and the doctor. Before the plane took off, however, he issued certain instructions, as a result of which the BAA 500 aircraft was replaced by another Delta, and the suspect machine was towed by tractor, under guard, into the Instecon hangar, where engineers began a methodical and meticulous scrutiny of every one of its parts. BAA accused Instecon of highhandedness, but the company lawyer waved a contract at them which gave Instecon the right to withdraw a Delta from service at any time without explanation, and reminded BAA of the long list of other airlines queueing for delivery of the plane.

When the Executive Delta touched down later that afternoon, Alec was driven across the field to the Instecon Office, where he was greeted by Customs and Immigration officers who cleared him for entry into the country. The doctor had been informed of his impending arrival, and they met in what had been Ross Compton's office.

'This is an odd one,' Dr Gervis said. 'I've already had two second opinions, from two consultant pathologists. So far as we can discover, Ross Compton died simply because his heart stopped beating.'

'No traces of poison, no violence . . .?'

'Absolutely nothing, and believe me, we've looked for everything. He was an abnormally healthy, well-developed, fit man. He neither smoked, nor drank, nor ate to excess. No evidence of drugs, and believe me, Professor Baxter is the authority on drugs – and poisons – he's just published the standard work on them we'll all be using for years . . .'

'Hypnotism?'

'I thought of that, too,' Dr Gervis said. 'In fact one of my first thoughts. But I've talked with Jack Landon, he's supposed to be the best in that particular field – and I asked him if it would be possible to hypnotize someone into holding his breath long enough to kill himself. Landon said it's impossible.'

'Where is Mr Compton now?'

'In the mortuary. We had to notify the police, of course,

but they're holding off for the moment. After all they have three medical reports to say he died from natural causes. His own doctor's been informed, of course, but he's had no reason to see Compton for five years, and so he can't issue a death certificate.'

'There'll be an inquest?'

'Open and shut. Death by Natural Causes.'

'Not, Causes Unknown?'

'Oh no. We'll tell the coroner Ross Compton died because his heart stopped. That's the cause of death.'

'And if the coroner asks you why the heart stopped?'

'We'll say we don't know . . .'

'Right, that takes care of the official side. But what's your personal opinion?'

'Did he die, or was he murdered? Is that what you're asking?'

'In a word, yes.'

'Look, Mr Haig, we're very far advanced with medical science, pathology, all the factual matters to do with the human body. But I still think there are many things we don't yet know. Ross Compton didn't just die. He was killed. I'm convinced of that. But – next question – who or what killed him? And there I would become very fanciful. When I say Ross Compton was killed, I mean his life was ended by some agency beyond our comprehension. Some *agency*. That could be the administration of an unknown poison by an unknown human being, but it could also be some demonic or Divine manipulation about which we know absolutely nothing . . .'

Dr Gervis stopped and looked embarrassed. 'I know doctors aren't supposed to give vent to these fanciful feelings,' he said apologetically, 'and possibly I'm just over-reacting to having seen that man die. It's not an experience to be treated lightly, to stand there and watch a man's life end, and know there's nothing you or anybody else can do about it . . .'

When the doctor had gone, Alec Haig walked along the perimeter road to the Instecon hangar, his mind buzzing with unanswered questions. Was Dr Gervis being fanciful? Had Ross Compton's life been ended *'by some agency'*? Ross himself had suspected something, or he would not have put out the special emergency call that had brought Alec all the way back from Hong Kong in such a hurry, and had grounded BAA's Delta. The plane was in the hangar, behind closed and guarded doors. Even though the guard recognized Alec Haig, he still asked him to submit to the identification procedures in the guard office. Alec placed his thumb against the panel of the scanner, which read his print and passed him. Inside, the engineers were swarming all over the plane, examining parts, checking assemblies and the working of the plane's many mechanisms. The Chief Service Engineer, who'd come from the Instecon factory in Hertfordshire, was talking to one of the engineers examining one of the parts. He brought the part across to Alec Haig when he recognized him. They went into the office together, and closed the door.

The Chief Service Engineer, George Mason, put the part on a sheet of clean white paper on the desk.

'I'm afraid we're on a wild goose-chase, Mr Haig,' he said. 'This is the thrust bearing, the one you sent the message about. We can't find anything wrong with it, and it was correctly installed. Charlie Lamport put it in, as you know, and Charlie's a good engineer. We've been over every inch of that plane, and frankly, I'd be happy to fly it to New York myself.'

'You've checked this bearing *completely*? Don't misunderstand me, I'm not suggesting it's been skimped . . .'

'We checked the installation. Perfect. Friction coefficient

41

exactly right, alignment, temperature under load, lubricant feed, everything. Then we flew the bearing by helicopter to Hertfordshire. We've just got it back. There they checked roller hardness, ring hardness, polish. They've examined the metal spectroscopically and analysed the lubricant. We can *guarantee* that bearing hasn't been tampered with, nothing is wrong with it.'

George Mason stood back from the desk and gestured for Alec to look at the bearing, almost defying him to find something wrong with it, as if the whole matter were a slur on his own professional status and reputation.

'What does Charlie Lamport say ...?' Alec asked, to mollify him. Engineers can be more sensitive than a *prima ballerina*.

'I don't know,' George Mason said, 'I haven't been able to talk to him. We sent a car to his house, but apparently, after he left work this morning, he didn't go home. I've got a driver waiting to bring him in the moment he arrives.'

'Take my word for it,' Alec Haig said. 'Your driver will be waiting a long time ...'

*　　　*　　　*

Ross Compton had lived in a detached house at High Wycombe. The lawn at the front of the house was tended with the precision of an engineer. The roses in the rose bed, no longer blooming, were lined with an almost mathematical precision. Mrs Compton came to the door; when Alec Haig told her he was from Instecon, she took him through to the long room which overlooked the front of the house. She had been crying, but now she had stopped.

'It's good of you to come,' she said, 'now I think of it, Ross mentioned your name several times. And Mr Mason. Chief Engineer, isn't he?'

'Head of Engineering for the Aviation Division. Your husband was one of his best men. Mine too.'

'I hadn't realized my husband worked for you. What's your department?'

'I'm Head of Technical Sales. Your husband helped me from time to time.'

'They still don't know what was wrong with him?'

'I'm afraid they don't.'

'That's what's so awful. I mean, not knowing what he died of. It'd be easier, somehow, if I could tell myself he had a weak heart, or high blood pressure, or anything you could put your finger on, but he was such a healthy man. He did all that gardening single handed you know ... And he played golf, and cricket, and tennis. And he was always going out for a run, or a long walk with the dog. Do you know, Mr Haig, my husband never had a moment's illness all the days I've known him ...'

She looked as if she was going to cry again. This part of his job Alec Haig didn't enjoy, but forced himself to do. Ross Compton had died because he was where Alec had put him. Of course the company would pay a pension to the widow. But they could not replace this woman's husband.

'I wanted you to know how much we all respected your husband,' Alec said, 'and how proud we are to have known him, and to have worked with him. Of course, you'll get a letter from the company, but I just wanted to come here and say that to you ...'

He could see she was grateful. 'It's very good of you,' she said. 'Somehow it makes it easier to know he was respected by other people ...' And she started to weep silently. Alec

Haig sat there, looking at her. 'Is there anything I can do,' he asked, 'anything you need? I hate to mention it, but are you all right for cash . . .?'

'Oh, yes, I'm all right,' she said. 'Ross was a careful man, and we had a joint account. I shall have to sell this house, of course, but I wouldn't want to stay here, now Ross has gone.'

'Then there's nothing I can do for you?'

'There is just one thing,' she said. 'It'd make it easier, somehow. I can't explain it, but I'd be happier in my mind if you could find out exactly why Ross died. Find that out for me, would you?'

'You can rest assured, I intend to do that very thing,' Alec Haig said grimly.

A suite had been rented for the use of Ben Thomas, Arthur Lovell, and Samy Brunel in the Associated Hotel in Park Lane. The Associated had been chosen because it had three banks of elevators, and two bars and a restaurant on the roof. Nobody going up in any of the lifts was ever questioned in the lobby. Unmarried couples and people doing secret deals found it very convenient. The suite had been rented in the name of Mr Copeland, and each week the bill was paid by post in cash.

It wasn't the only bill to be paid that way at the Associated.

Charlie Lamport used elevator bank three to the twenty-seventh floor, as he'd been instructed. The elevator opened on to the restaurant, where breakfast was already being served. He came out of the elevator, then tapped his pockets as if absent-minded and went down in the elevator again. This time, he stopped at the twenty-fourth floor, turned left out of the elevator, and walked along the corridor a few paces. The door of the suite was almost opposite the end of the bank of elevators; he rang the doorbell, waited until the door was opened from the inside, and went in. Samy was standing behind the opened door. He shut the door hurriedly behind Charlie, then followed him down the short corridor past the bathroom and the clothes cupboard into the sitting-room. Arthur Lovell was waiting there, with Ben Thomas, both wearing dressing-gowns over pyjamas. Through the opened bedroom door Charlie could see the two unmade beds, though the settee bed on which Samy must have slept was undisturbed.

They looked at Charlie. He bit his fingers nervously.

'Want some coffee?' Arthur Lovell asked, but Charlie shook his head. 'I'd like to get off home as soon as I can,' he said. 'If I could just have my money.'

'It worked all right?' Ben asked.

Charlie nodded.

'When did you give it to him?'

'In his coffee, when we were having breakfast, like you said. Only one thing, though, I was a bit nervous, and he only left me for a moment, and I tipped the whole lot in.'

'Double dose, eh? That's bad . . .'

Samy was standing behind Charlie, and slightly to his left. He shook his head warningly at Ben, confident Charlie couldn't see him. 'What about the check?' he asked quietly.

Charlie turned to look at him, licking his lips, then gnawing again at a thumbnail. 'It worked as you said it would. He was on the ball for the first two pages, but after that he was, like, in a daze. I had to keep reminding him to put the tick on the page. The first time I called a wrong reading was half-way down page three. The oil pressure on the left-hand forward baffle plate mechanism. Should be fifty pounds per square inch, plus or minus ten per cent . . .'

'We know that,' Arthur Lovell growled, 'but what did you call out?'

'Five hundred pounds per square inch.'

'And he accepted it?'

'Without question.'

'And made his tick . . .?'

'Yes.'

'Just as a point of interest,' Ben asked, 'what was the oil pressure reading? The real one?'

'Fifty-one point five pounds per square inch. Well within the tolerance. I had been a bit worried; we'd changed a bearing but it must have bedded down all right. Look, I can't see the point of all this, you know. I can't see the point of doping him, and calling out the wrong numbers. We know there's nothing wrong with the plane . . .'

'Don't you worry about that aspect of it,' Samy said reassuringly. 'You don't think we'd want to damage a Delta, do you? We're testing a drug, and you're being very helpful to us. The company won't forget it . . .'

Charlie still looked doubtful. 'Don't you understand,' Samy said, 'it's most important that Ross Compton doesn't know the drug's been given to him, or we shan't get a correct result for the medical men . . . it has to be done this way, secretly.'

'But I can't understand all this messing about. Why can we only meet here, and not at the works? Why did I have to check into a room on the next floor up? Under a false name? Why . . .'

46

'You worry too much, Charlie,' Samy said. 'Anyway, you're being paid well for the overtime, aren't you . . .'

'Can I have the two hundred,' Charlie said. 'I've got to get home.'

'The money's waiting for you. In your room. Now it looks to me as if you need a cup of coffee so drink this down and then go and collect your money and that can be the end of it so far as you're concerned, can't it?'

Charlie drank the coffee and went up one flight to the room into which he had checked the previous afternoon. Samy came with him. The drug they'd put into the coffee worked just as Charlie opened the door. Samy lifted him into the room, stripped him, dumped him under the shower and turned the water full on at its maximum heat. It took Charlie fifteen minutes to die by which time all traces of the poison had been expelled from his body by the heat of the scalding water.

Samy went downstairs. The other two were dressed and waiting for him. They put their personal effects and clothing into the briefcases they carried, left the suitcase packed with nondescript and untraceable clothing in the sitting-room of the suite. From a telephone booth in the lobby, Samy rang the hotel number, checked out 'Mr Copeland' and asked that his luggage be put in store. The room rent had been paid up to twelve o'clock that day and, so far as Associated was concerned, the transaction was perfectly normal and unnoteworthy.

Anyway, the hotel had more to worry about than that. A chambermaid had just discovered in the shower in room 2512 the naked body of a man who appeared to have died of a heart attack due to turning the water on too hot. A Señor Enrique Castello, from Buenos Aires, according to his booking-in card. The only thing the clerk could remember about him was that he'd spoken quite good English, for a foreigner . . .

*　　*　　*

Fact number one, Alec thought. Ross Compton, a man not given to hysteria, believing he'd been poisoned or drugged had invoked emergency procedures to communicate immediately with Security. Ross had also suspected the plane had been tampered with, or had been inadequately serviced. Fact number two; Ross Compton had died.

But fact number three; eminent and unimpeachable medical experts were prepared to swear in a coroner's court that Ross had died of heart stoppage for which they could locate no medical or pathological cause, and George Mason the Chief Engineer, beyond reproach, had sworn that the plane had not been tampered with, and had been correctly serviced. Fact number five; Charlie Lamport appeared to have vanished.

But was any one of these facts significant? The doctor had said he believed a man can die by other than human agency. Had Ross any grounds for his suspicions? Charlie Lamport hadn't gone home, but was that fact significant? Might he not be involved in some sort of personal crisis? Or perhaps a traffic hold-up, or even a traffic accident? Was this a *wild-goose chase*? Sir Barton Underwood always said Alec had a nose for trouble, and to Alec this situation had an indefinable odour. But of what?

'Can I put the Delta back into service?' George Mason asked.

Alec nodded. He couldn't keep the plane grounded without adequate reason. 'Fancy a trip?' he asked.

'I was going to suggest something like that,' George Mason said. 'I'll get BAA to put it on the New York flight, and travel with them.'

They had brought Alec's Wolseley to the airport, and he drove it alone into central London, where he kept a small flat in a block above the Grosvenor Cinema in Mayfair. When he arrived the telephone was ringing, but it was a wrong number. He poured himself a gin and tonic from the cupboard in the sitting-room, went into the bedroom, stripped and took a shower. Still the worry niggled at his mind, an inner conviction something had been missed, something was wrong. It was eleven o'clock at night, and had started to rain. He stood at the window, another drink in his hand, and looked down into the street below. Cars moved slowly along, waiting to drop their passengers at the clubs with which the street was lined. A policeman was walking slowly down the other side of the street; when she saw him coming a girl, who had been waiting in a doorway, turned and walked rapidly down the street past him. By the way the policeman waved his hand Alec guessed the girl had said goodnight to him. The phone rang again. Alec picked it up. It was another wrong number.

Alec put down the telephone, poured himself another drink. 'Dammit, that's the third,' he said to himself, and left the drink untouched. He went to bed, but couldn't sleep, tossed and turned in the bed growing hotter and hotter beneath the blankets. He turned on the radio beside his bed, and tuned it to the Overseas Service of the BBC. The time was three fifteen. Ilsa had just finished reading the news. The switchboard operator, bright as a button even at that hour, connected Alec with the studio. He heard the programme go off the air with a final announcement of the wavelengths on which the programme would be broadcast 'at the same time tomorrow', and then Ilsa picked up the telephone.

'That was a good programme,' Alec said.

'Who is this, please?'

'One of your listeners . . .'

'You bastard . . .'

'You recognized my voice.'

'God knows how. It's so long since I've heard it.'

'My stomach is still on Hong Kong time. Can I buy you breakfast?'

'In London, at this time of night? Or are you going to whisk me off to Paris again, so we can eat croissants in the Place du Tertre, and sip Calvados? I've missed you, you bastard . . .'

'Don't keep calling me that; my parents really were married, you know. There's a cab-driver's place in Fleet Street . . .'

'Where are you ringing from?'

'My place.'

'Yes, you bastard, but which one? Zürich, London . . .?'

'London.'

'Still the same place, above the cinema?'

'Yes.'

'Start me a bath and I'll be over in ten minutes, if I can find a cab at this ungodly hour.'

'I can come to pick you up.'

'You still accept my thumbprint on the door.'

'Yes – of course. I *could* come and pick you up . . .'

'Save your strength,' Ilsa said. 'It's been a long time since I've seen you, you bastard.'

✳   ✳   ✳

Five minutes later when Alec had started the water running, poured perfumed essence into the bath, put two glasses into the freezer to chill for the martinis he was making, and switched the pad in the bed to 'low heat' to take the chill from the sheets, the phone rang again.

This time it was not a wrong number.

'Dr Gervis asked me to call you,' Professor Baxter explained. 'He said you wouldn't mind what time it was. I've found something interesting in this matter of your man Compton.'

When Ilsa arrived ten minutes later she found the bath full, the coffee percolating and a note from Alec. 'Very sorry, but alas I must dash out. I hope to be back soon.'

'You bastard,' she said as she helped herself to the coffee and prepared for a long, slow bath.

Professor Baxter's laboratory was in the basement of a house in Wimpole Street. The front door was unlocked and the front hall smelled of wax polish and central heating. Alec went across as instructed, through the door straight ahead which opened on to a staircase going down. Here the air smelled of formalin and pine disinfectant, twin odours of health and death. Professor Baxter was waiting at the bottom of the stairs, a short chubby man with rosy cheeks and the look of an impertinent schoolboy in the twinkle of his eyes. He was wearing an immaculate white laboratory coat, from the top pocket of which a pair of long scissors protruded. As he preceded Alec into the laboratory, he walked with a pronounced limp. Alec looked down quickly, and saw the Professor's left boot had a platform sole and heel. On any other man the limp would have added a sinister touch; it made the Professor seem, somehow, more human and more vulnerable.

'You've had a busy night,' Alec said. The Professor took

Alec's light raincoat and hung it in a cupboard near the door. 'I work best when it's quiet,' he said, 'when the lab people aren't about, and the telephone doesn't ring. I'm afraid there are going to be a few red faces in the morning. Not least my own. Professional men don't like admitting they are wrong, that they have overlooked something. We made a report, three of us, certifying we had found nothing toxic in the body of your Mr Compton. That report was true in substance. We had *found* nothing toxic. We have committed the error of assuming that means nothing toxic was there.'

'And now you've found something, toxic?'

'Yes, I have.'

'I'd like to know what caused you to go on looking, even after you'd submitted a report.'

'That excessive perspiration. It worried me,' Professor Baxter said. He led Alec across the laboratory to where a couple of seats had been placed, next to a bench on which was a microscope, a number of slides, and test-tubes in racks. Alec seated himself, and glanced round the room, which was spotlessly clean – a place for everything, and everything in its place. 'How much do you know about poisons?' Professor Baxter asked him.

'Not a lot.'

'You know that there exists a group of poisons which affects the nervous system?'

'I have heard that.'

'Usually we can find traces of such poisons in the body of the victim after death. As you know, we analysed everything to do with Mr Compton, and found no traces of any foreign substance either in his stomach or his digestive tract, his bowels or his bladder.' Alec wondered at this cheerful little man who, in pursuit of an elusive idea, had spent his night in what could only have been a most gruesome and unpleasant analysis. 'We'd even taken scrapings of the perspiration of the surface of the man's skin, and they proved to be entirely negative . . .'

'You've gone to a lot of trouble . . .'

'It's not trouble, my dear chap. It's a fascinating problem. Of course even with the clue of perspiration in the normal course of events, I'd have still said there was no possibility the man Compton had been poisoned, and quite cheerfully have left it at that . . .'

'But you persisted? Why?'

'Entirely because of Doctor Gervis. He gave me some twaddle about death being possible by Divine intervention. I'm an atheist by conviction, and I can't have a chap like Gervis slipping anything like that past me. Damn it, he'd have had me believing in God, next. So I persisted. I wanted to find this 'Divine intervention', and I think that's just what I've done. It was in the perspiration, you see. Perspiration carries a lot of the body substance with it. This poison escapes from the body with the perspiration. It causes an enormous rise in body temperatures, the sweat glands open, and the poison works itself out of the system. When we get a corpse to examine, we have to move it about quite a bit in the unclothed state, and most of the perspiration dries out. That doesn't usually matter, since when the perspiration evaporates and the body dries, a small amount of salts is left on the skin, sufficient for us to take a scrape for analysis. That was what we'd done. We'd scraped the skin and had analysed the salts. No traces of anything known, no arsenic, none of the organic poisons like strychnine and so forth. But by chance Mr Compton's body hadn't been moved about too much, and when I lifted his left arm, I found a drop of perspiration remaining under his arm-pit. His left arm-pit. It was only one drop, but sufficient for my purposes.'

'And that was the poison . . .?'

'It contained a minute amount of a highly toxic substance. Have you heard of those ampoules of amyl nitrite they give to a certain type of heart patient? If the patient feels an attack coming on, he breaks the tip of the ampoule in a handkerchief and sniffs the amyl nitrite; this causes his heart to race. One side effect is that the patient flushes, and perspires heavily. Well, this substance is a derivative of amyl nitrite, very similar in its actions, and completely organic. It would be evacuated completely from the body via the sweat glands within a matter of an hour, and no trace of it would be discoverable.'

'Unless a little of it was trapped say under the victim's arm-pit?'

'That's right. It would be most unusual for that to happen. When the poison is administered, the victim is clothed. The clothing absorbs the underarm perspiration, and the poison evaporates from the clothing, leaving no trace behind. We were lucky in this case that the body was undressed before the perspiration had evaporated and that arm wasn't moved about as much as is normal in a post-mortem . . .'

'We were also lucky in having a persistent pathologist . . .'

'Yes, I will take a little credit for that,' Professor Baxter said, chuckling, 'though you must really give thanks to God and Dr Gervis . . .'

Alec seated himself on a chair in the laboratory. 'This poison, Professor Baxter, does it have a name?'

'It has a chemical name, of course, not that the name would help you much. It's nitromethylethyloxy . . .'

Alec held up his hand. 'I didn't mean the chemical name,' he said, 'I wondered if it had a trade name.'

'No, it has no trade name. So far as I know, it's not made

commercially for any reason, and thank God, so far, we have no evidence of its being used as a poison.'

'Can you tell me what its effect would be . . . ?'

'Well, it would lift your body temperature. Possibly give you increased heart activity, push up your pulse rate. You'd sweat. That would be the outward sign . . .'

'And inwardly . . . ?'

'This is something we don't know too much about, of course, but it has been used, I believe, for selective purposes. You see, it can knock out one part of your nervous system and keep the other parts functioning correctly. You could probably walk and talk and laugh, just like a normal human being. If you were threatened in any way, shall we say, if someone tried to punch you, you'd be perfectly capable of taking avoiding action . . .'

'But all this time, a part of you would be missing . . . ?'

'Yes, that's it. That's what I mean by selective. It "selects" a part of your nervous system, and neutralizes it for a short time . . .'

'How short a time?'

'You realize we haven't done too many experiments with this particular substance, so I'm afraid I can't give you a scientific answer. It could be minutes, it could be hours. Each case would depend on the amount administered, how long it took for the system of the body to expel it via perspiration, body temperature, the ambient temperature, the amount and kind of physical activity. Any of these factors would influence the time of effectiveness . . .'

'You said the drug was "selective". Can you say which part of the system it would select?'

'That again is something I'd hate to predict without more research. It would be the same part each time, of course since each of these drugs works in a biochemical way, acting on one

55

part of the chemistry of the nervous system. But specifically which part, I'm afraid it would be impossible for me to say. Of course, if you would care to take a sample of the drug, and let one of my psychiatric friends examine you under its influence . . .'

Alec Haig laughed, but it was an uneasy sound. There had been times he'd been compelled to use himself as a guinea-pig . . . But not with an unknown drug.

'Side effects . . .?'

'Impossible to predict, again without years of research.'

'Effects of an overdose . . .?'

'Now this is something that worries me, in relation to Mr Compton. The effects of an overdose should be clearly marked; it should accelerate the heart's activities rather like driving an engine at too high a speed. In the case of an engine, the piston rings or the valves would go. Something would actually mechanically break. The same should be true of the heart. If you overstimulated it, something physical would happen, and we'd be able to see it. But Compton's heart is, in every sense, perfect, with no sign of physical damage.'

'Let me put a hypothesis to you,' Alec said. 'A man conducts a number of activities as a part of a routine. All he needs to do physically is to read a number of dials, and then make a mark on a pad. Of course, when he reads the dials his critical ability comes into play and if what the dial tells him is wrong, he doesn't make the tick . . .'

'Let me interrupt you there,' Professor Baxter said. 'When you say, if what the dial tells him is "wrong" are you implying a moral decision? Or merely a departure from the norm . . .?'

Alec thought for a minute. 'No, I don't think it's a moral question,' he said, 'merely a departure from the norm. But as an engineer, any such departure implies something is wrong.'

'But what happens,' Professor Baxter said, 'just for the sake of your hypothesis, if there is no norm? If the drug has, so to speak, wiped out the part of the memory which deals with norms? That's really what we're dealing with, isn't it? Your man – and I assume you mean Mr Compton – is accustomed to looking at dials and seeing certain figures. I look at the dial on my motor car and see my fuel meter has an arrow pointing to the letter "E" and my memory is invoked to remind me that if I don't do something I shall not continue to have the use of that vehicle. The fuel meter establishes a "norm" which I follow instinctively. I also have another meter on my dashboard, which tells me if my battery is being charged or not . . .'

'An ammeter.'

'Well, it may surprise you to know that I hate the innards of a motor car with a fierce and passionate loathing, and frankly I don't *want* to know what an ammeter does, and therefore that ammeter could be registering all the wrong facts, and I would not be aware of any implication . . . My memory, you see, has been "tuned out" by my hatred of motor-car mechanics. Now, to return to your Mr Compton, he could sit there looking at his dials, and under the influence of this drug, he wouldn't give a damn what the dials were reading, because he wouldn't have a "memory" of any normality. It would have been "tuned out" by the drug . . .'

'But he'd still continue to make ticks?'

'Most probably, yes. Because his physical activity would be unaffected by the drug. To all intents and purposes, he'd behave quite normally. If he was a smoking man, he'd want a cigarette and be perfectly capable of taking one, lighting it, and smoking it . . .'

'And enjoying it . . .?'

'I can't go so far as to say that. Enjoyment depends on

memory.' Both sat silent, thinking of Ross Compton reading the dials and making ticks on the paper no matter what alarm those dials were screaming at him. Alec knew Charlie Lamport had been sitting beside Ross and could visualize the scene in the cockpit of the plane. Did Charlie Lamport still bite his fingernails, he asked himself irrelevantly. Charlie Lamport had disappeared, and Ross Compton had died, and the Chief Engineer had certified nothing had been wrong with the plane. In all probability, the dials had fed the correct message back to both Ross and Charlie, and each tick had been justified. If nothing was wrong with the plane, however, why had the drug been administered? It now seemed clear to Alec that Charlie had probably doped Ross when they were having breakfast together. Hadn't Ross said he'd left the table to get the sugar bowl, or was it the cream jug? It didn't matter why he'd left the table; Charlie Lamport had an opportunity to slip a quantity of the drug into Ross's food or drink.

'You don't think the drug killed Mr Compton?' he asked.

Professor Baxter's cheerful face twinkled, his eyes were merry. 'How does he do it?' Alec thought. It was five o'clock in the morning and Alec was dropping from fatigue. It had been a long day, starting with a demanding and busy half-day in Hong Kong, a quarter of the way round the world. No doubt Professor Baxter had also had a busy day, but he was still completely active, completely in charge of all his faculties. 'No, I don't think the drug killed your man,' Professor Baxter said. 'I'm reminded of the words of Francis Bacon in his essay on Death – *I don't believe any man fears to be dead, but only the stroke of Death*. Mr Compton suspected something was wrong when he found himself sweating excessively. At that time, don't forget, he was sufficiently in control of his faculties to arrange to telephone you, even though you were in Hong Kong. From what I've been told, he used a special code, so his memory must have been quite unimpaired at that time. He even sent for a doctor, using the same code. I have no doubt that, at that moment, any memory-killing attributes of this drug had already worn off. But the perspiration would continue to flow for a time while the drug was expelling itself from his system. He wasn't to know that, of course. He found himself getting hotter and hotter, wetter and wetter. He knew a drug had been administered to him. He didn't know the drug was harmless and that its worst effects were already over. He thought he'd been poisoned. When the doctor spoke to you on the telephone, he told you he could locate no traces of a drug. Not immediately and superficially, anyway. I believe that Ross Compton took that to mean a poison had been administered which was going to be difficult, possibly even impossible, to analyse and neutralize.'

'But he didn't die of the drug . . .?'

'No. Quite simply, I believe he died of fright.'

Ilsa was in bed and asleep when Alec returned to his flat shortly after six o'clock, which was just as well. No sooner had Alec taken off his raincoat, poured himself a cup of coffee, glanced in the bedroom and seen Ilsa's sleeping form, than the telephone began ringing.

'Hold on,' the operator said, 'I have a call for you from New York.'

Alec held on and after a lot of what sounded like early

morning bird-song and cats being tortured, he heard a voice
he instantly recognized. 'I'm just going to bed, but I imagine
you're just getting up for a run round the park,' George
Phillimore said. 'One thing I just simply love about London
is a run round the park in the early morning . . .'

'Come off it, you night owl,' Alec said, 'you've never seen
an early morning in your life . . . Now what about my
shares?'

The line crackled with silence then. 'I don't know how to
tell you this, Alec,' George said, 'and even yet I don't know
myself what it means, but those shares of yours are going to
be hell to unload. Believe me, I've talked to everybody, but
everybody, and nobody wants 'em.'

'You saw the New York closing price . . .?'

'Sure, and it's great: 308. What's more, I've just seen the
San Francisco closing prices, and Instecon International has
held, closing at 308.04. But you know who's buying, Alec.
Not the big boys, but the little guys, the people who've
always wanted a few thousand but never had the chance to
buy them because the big boys were sitting tight. So we have
a problem, Alec. If I put your shares on the market, and
they're broken down into small lots, that's bound to bring
the price down. I could get rid of them very easily over say
the next thirty days, a few at a time, but it'd be suicide to
dump them, Alec. I had hoped to get one buyer to pick up
the lot, but that's what's killing me. Not one of the institutions is interested. So what gives, Alec? Isn't it time you
started levelling with me? I can see now why you needed to
play this one close to your chest, but believe me, Alec, I need
to know what the hell's going on if I'm going to help you.
Let's forget all that crap about selling your shares. You
never wanted to sell them in the first place. You wanted me
to find out exactly what I have found out, that on the big

board, it's no dice so far as International Instecon is concerned, right?'

'Right,' Alec said. He had to trust George Phillimore, if he was going to get any help from him. George would play it close to his chest, would only act in Alec's best interests. Instecon was too big even for George to play ducks and drakes with.

'Okay, okay,' George said. 'Now get this. Tomorrow you're in for one helluva bad time, unless you get off your ass and do something about it. You know Sam Bantam?'

'I know him.'

'Well Sam, you may not know, acts as investment counsellor to a number of blue chip companies . . .'

'I did know that . . .'

'Well, here's something you don't know. I just talked with Sam Bantam. Tried to sound him out about your shares in fact. And Sam gave me the horse laugh . . .'

The 'blue chip' companies Sam advised held well over a couple of million shares of Instecon International between them.

'And that's not all he gave me,' George said. 'He also advised me, man to man, the left hand washes the right, to get rid of any of your paper I'm holding when the New York Market opens tomorrow, and that, buddy-boy, is in ten hours' time.'

'Did he give you any reason why?'

'Yes, but it might not be ethical of me to tell you . . .'

'In that case, just nod your head if I come up with the right guess,' Alec said grimly, 'and I'll hear your brains creaking. Sam had control of over a couple of million Instecon International shares. When the market opens tomorrow morning, he proposes to dump 'em . . .?'

'You're calling the shots,' George said.

'And to use a bit of old-fashioned New York jargon, I'm the one who's sitting behind the eight ball . . .?'

'That's right,' George said. 'If you can find anyone who'll give you 250/60 for your shares when the London market opens, I'd recommend you take it. That way, you'll just beat Sam Bantam to the punch . . .'

'Why isn't he using the London market?'

'It's not his money, and he's on vacation. In Jamaica, with a broad.'

The note Alec had left for Ilsa was on the table. He looked into the bedroom. Ilsa had not moved in her sleep. He took out his pen and wrote another note. 'Please forgive me,' the note read, 'but I have to go away again. I'll ring you when I get back . . .'

He took the note into the bedroom and placed it on the bedside cabinet where Ilsa would see it when she woke. She stirred in her sleep, her body moving sensuously beneath the blankets. She must have been dreaming. 'You bastard,' she said quietly, not waking, a smile of pleasure on her face.

Alec went back into the living-room, picked up the telephone and dialled a number.

'I shall want the Delta ready to leave as soon as possible, but certainly not later than in an hour and a half. File a flight plan for Montego Bay, Jamaica. And dammit!'

'I beg your pardon, Mr Haig?' the operator said.

*　　　*　　　*

Ben Thomas had started his annual holiday and had told his colleagues he was going to Wales for a two-weeks walking holiday. 'Where can we find you if we need you?' his section boss asked, but Ben smiled at him.

'You can't,' he said. 'Unless you're prepared to climb all over the Black Mountains, calling for me . . .'

Arthur Lovell had started his annual holiday. A two-weeks coach tour of the West Country. 'One of the attractions of this holiday,' he told his workmates, 'is that you never know where you're going to turn up next. A two-week mystery tour . . . just the job for anyone who reports at the works at the same time every day . . .'

Samy Brunel said goodbye to the staff at the Aviation factory in Hertfordshire. 'I shan't be sorry to get back to France,' he said, 'your opening hours and your English bread are killing me.'

They met quite openly on the cross-channel ferry-boat from Harwich to the Hook of Holland, sat at the same table for lunch, and talked quite freely. The boat was only half full, and the other passengers were holiday-makers who had no interest in what went on around the other tables.

'So, it works?' Samy said, 'and now we must decide when and where.'

'I bloody well told you it would work,' Arthur said. His had been the bright idea for a way in which they could bring a plane out of the sky and still make it look like a design fault. They could interfere with a part of the tailplane assembly. The effect on the plane would be to make it lose electric power, even from its own generating systems. At a fixed point in the flight suddenly and quite without warning the plane would be crippled. The only snag, however, was that the fault would show during the pre-flight check on a meter used only by the engineers; that particular test wasn't part of the pilot's own pre-take-off check.

It was Samy who discovered and obtained the drug that

63

had been used so successfully on Ross Compton; it had been part of the research of the aviation medical centre at Toulouse, when they had studied the effects of various drugs on passengers; in 1968 a passenger had gone aboard an aircraft loaded with LSD and the altitude and pressure had made him go berserk. When Arthur Lovell 'invented' his method of crippling the plane, Samy remembered the drug that knocked a convenient hole in people's memories, and realized it could be used on the engineers to make them certify a plane as airworthy despite an obvious fault. Ross Compton had been the first guinea-pig, though they had left the plane intact in case the drug hadn't worked as it should.

At the Hook of Holland, they disembarked from the boat with the tourists, and climbed aboard the train for Amsterdam. They separated on the train. In Amsterdam, they went separately to the terminal and took the bus to Schiphol airport.

From there they took a KLM flight. To Rome.

PHASE 5

The airport at Montego Bay, Jamaica, is built on the coast-line, with an easy run in over the sea. The porters at the airport wear military-style shorts and shirts, and stand to attention in a line until the passenger baggage is unloaded. No scrambling for bags in the undignified manner of most airports throughout the world. Sip a rum, courtesy of the Jamaica Tourist Board, wait for your baggage to arrive, be cleared through Customs, and loaded into the car chosen for you by the policeman on duty. Landing at Montego Bay is one of the few pleasures left to travellers in this age of airport jumble and confusion.

When the private Instecon Delta touched down in Montego Bay, it caused a minor sensation on two counts. Firstly it had never landed there before, and instructions had to be relayed from the Delta's own computer to the control tower and back to the plane. Secondly, the Instecon Delta brought only one passenger.

Alec Haig.

The chief porter met him as he came through the door, took the briefcase which was his only baggage and carried it to the chief Customs inspector, who opened it, examined its contents solemnly, and then drew a chalk mark on its label, not wishing to soil the exquisite leather of the briefcase itself. The chief porter escorted Alec Haig into the outer hall, where he handed the briefcase to Willie. Willie smiled, but he didn't speak. He took the briefcase in his hand and opened the back door of the Lincoln Continental. The air conditioner had been working, and the interior of the car was cool in contrast to the heat of the airport. Then Willie came round to the front of the car, got in, and the car drove away from the airport buildings. When they had passed the roundabout at the airport entrance, Alec smiled.

'Well, Willie, how've you been?' he said.

Willie turned and smiled at him, a warm and affectionate greeting. 'I bin just fine, Mr Haig, just fine.'

'Car running okay?'

'Just fine, Mr Haig.'

'And I suppose your mother's just fine, and your father's just fine, and all your children are just fine, and when are you going to get married . . .?'

'When I find me a wife who's just fine, Mr Haig. Anyway, when you gonna get married, again, sah?'

'One of these days I'm going to surprise you.'

It was a bone of contention between them. Alec had been married, had brought his young bride to honeymoon in Jamaica. Willie had fallen for her instantly, had been at her beck and call. Mrs Haig had been the finest lady he had ever known, or so he said. But now she was dead, and Willie hoped every time Alec came to Jamaica, he'd bring a new wife with him.

He drove down the road both had been down many times before, to the Casa Negra, an old unspoiled family hotel only a hundred yards along the coast from a superb beach. Alerted by the Instecon central switchboard, Willie had reserved Alec Haig's usual three rooms, each with a second balcony hanging over the deep green water of the Caribbean. Willie had brought the suitcases he kept for Mr Haig, containing the socks and shirts and underwear all recently laundered, and the tropical-weight suits all recently pressed, and they were waiting in the centre room.

'Is Mr Haig expecting more guests?' the doorman asked. He was new at the hotel. 'You'll learn,' Willie said. 'Mr Haig likes his privacy . . .'

Willie was combined chauffeur, batman, bodyguard and information service to Alec and Jacques de Blaie whenever they came to Jamaica. When they were away, Willie drove the air-conditioned Lincoln Continental Alec had bought for him as a private hire car, taking rich people around the island, to and from the night clubs and golf courses and hotels, keeping his eyes and ears open. Kingston, Ocho Rios, Montego Bay, no matter where an important person stayed on the island, in a hotel or a private estate, Willie could be guaranteed to hear about him, to store knowledge to give to Mr Haig should ever he need it. And with half the rich industrialists of Europe and America taking winter holidays on the island paradise, Alec could often make use of the snippets Willie provided.

'Where's Mr Bantam, Willie?' Alec asked when the doorman had gone.

Willie cackled, slapped his leg with amusement, his shiny black face creased even more with amusement.

'Mr Bantam, sah, de laughing stock of de whole island. Mr Bantam, sah, he bring de *Liberty Belle* and anchor her off de yacht club in Montego Bay, and step ashore nice and sprightly, and never set foot on de boat again . . .'

'Why not, Willie, the crocodiles get him?'

'Yes, sir, in a manner of speaking, yes, sir. Only one crocodile, and she as pretty as anything you ever saw in and out of de water. We call her de White Lady. What for she come to Jamaica if she never go in de sunshine? But Mr Bantam, sah, he like de White Lady, and so de *Liberty Belle* she moored off de Montego Bay Yacht club, and she fit to sink to de bottom of de ocean.'

It was a characteristic of Willie, indeed of Jamaicans in general, that everything had a life and a personality. Willie could conceive of a boat like the *Liberty Belle*, pining away at her moorings while her master neglected her for the charms of this mysterious 'White Lady'.

'Who is the White Lady?' Alec asked.

'Doan't ask me,' Willie said, rolling his eyes, 'she got a name I couldn't pronounce nohow.'

'Can't you tell me anything about her? Where is she staying? A hotel, an estate? Who's she staying with? Come on, Willie, I'm in a hurry.'

Willie became all business, dropped his comical Black Sambo act. 'She came to de island with Mr Fritz von Heppeldorf, sah, in de private plane, but when Mr Heppeldorf done go back to Europe she done stay on de island, in de Crescent Moon Hotel. And Mr Bantam come to de island and de first day she send a boy from de Crescent Moon to Mr Bantam's boat, sah, and in three days, or maybe I should say three nights, sah, Mr Bantam done rented de Frobisher Place and paid de White Lady's bill at de Crescent Moon and day done moved in together. And de lady don't like de sunshine, not nohow, and I doan't know what she doing to Mr Bantam but he ain't never going sailing in de *Liberty Belle*, not with de White Lady. Not nohow.'

'Fritz von Heppeldorf, eh?' Alec said, musing. 'I don't keep up with the love lives of these playboys, but the last thing I heard he had Miss Calabria in tow, or was she Miss Acapulco? What did she call herself, Veronica something or other . . .'

'That's right, sah, Veronica, but doan't ask me to pronounce de rest of it. That's why we call her de White Lady.'

So Sam Bantam had shacked up with Veronica, former Miss Calabria or Acapulco, Fritz von Heppeldorf's cast-off. At his age he ought to have known better, though it must be flattering to have a young girl make eyes at you, Alec thought, when you're approaching fifty, your hair is thinning on top, and your chest has slipped below your waist-line . . .

'Anything known about Veronica, Willie?' Alec asked.

Willie looked at him for a moment, wondering how far he could go. White men are strange. They treat a black man as if he's okay most of the time, but suddenly, wham!

'House-boy at de Crescent Moon say she white all over, Mr Haig, and she very lonely when Mr Heppeldorf leave her.'

Sometimes Alec didn't like what he did. This was one of them. Other people's morals were not his concern. What Sam Bantam did, what this mysterious 'White Lady' did, was not his business, other than to know if their conduct might influence the affairs of Instecon, the organization whose survival was being threatened. Once that story hit the market, the value of Instecon would drop faster than a chorine's mini-skirt. Alec knew that Instecon was as sound as any company, well managed, well-run, a secure investment for anybody's money. But the company was being threatened and undermined in the worst possible way, by rumour and ill-founded gossip. Men like Sam Bantam could bring the company to its knees if nothing was done to check them and Alec knew it was his duty to use any fact, any information to preserve his company's good name. His first action when he arrived in Montego Bay was to send a telegram to the Instecon Head Office in Zürich. They'd think he'd gone out of his head if they weren't already quite accustomed to his strange requests. But he'd never asked for a complete dossier on a beauty queen before . . .

One of the great advantages of flying the Delta was that,

at a thousand miles an hour, the passenger seemed to arrive before he had left when he travelled in a westerly direction. It was still only seven o'clock local time when he had sent the cable to Zürich, and the New York market would not move for another four hours. Though Alec had slept only three hours on the plane he arrived perfectly refreshed; he stripped and put on his swimming trunks and trudged through the water off Doctor's Cave for a quarter of an hour in the hot Jamaican November sunshine. Few people were about at that time of morning, and the coffee shop had not yet opened. He went back to his room, changed into a light-weight suit and silk shirt, and ate a quick breakfast of paw-paw, cornflakes, and bacon. Then he set out with Willie in the Lincoln Continental for the Frobisher Place, along the coast road not far from Rose Hall.

Frobisher was a diamond tycoon who had built a two-storey house on the north coast of the island of Jamaica in the late thirties, on a hundred and fifty acres of which a quarter of a mile was a completely secluded bay with white crystal sand along a crescent fifty yards wide in the centre. At one end of the crescent Frobisher had excavated a deep harbour and in the high living days had moored an ocean-going yacht there, when it wasn't off Cannes, or Monte Carlo. The Frobisher Place, as it was always called with some local contempt, had been the scene of wild parties all through the late thirties. Frobisher himself was a wild gambling man – baccarat, *chemin de fer*, poker, roulette – and many were the legends of him winning and losing tens of thousands of pounds at a session. His reputation was established one night in Monte Carlo in 1936 when, with maximum table stakes on every possible bet on the number five, the number had repeated itself no less than six times. Frobisher, so legend had it, left the table with over a quarter of a million pounds. Legend didn't report, however, that Frobisher had lost double that amount the following night, playing *chemin de fer* against the Greek, Zardanopolous.

When Frobisher was killed in the British Army in 1940, he was found to owe more than two million pounds. Since then the Frobisher Place in Jamaica had passed from hand to hand, and now it was rumoured that an American hotel chain planned to purchase it and develop the idyllic site for low-priced holidays. The Jamaicans had mixed feelings about that; it would bring in thousands of tourists each year, but they would be the low-class low-spenders and the exclusiveness and high prices of food and entertainment along the north coast would tumble.

Meanwhile the Frobisher place was owned by a mixed Jamaican/British/Bahamanian Syndicate, and available for rental.to anyone who could pay two thousand pounds sterling a month and didn't mind its somewhat tarnished reputation. Sam Bantam could pay the rent out of what he normally carried in his back pocket, and was reputed to earn never less than half a million dollars a year. When Alec arrived, the Jamaican house-boy Tobias asked him to wait while he looked to see if the master was 'in'; Alec gave him a personal card engraved with the Sutton Place South, New York, address and no company identification, and was promptly ushered through to the terrace. Sam was sitting there eating a grapefruit and drinking coffee; he was wearing white linen shorts and a flowered Hawaiian shirt which failed to hide his dropped waist-line. He got up, offered Alec coffee when they shook hands, and they sat down together. Alec insisted Sam finish his breakfast, but when Tobias arrived with boiled eggs, Sam waved him away.

'What line of business you in, Mr Haig?' he asked.

Alec smiled at him, pleasantly. So that was the way Sam

wanted to play it. He knew damn well who and what Alec Haig was, though it was doubtful he knew Alec's special responsibility for Security. So far as he knew, Alec was on the board of Instecon International as Technical Sales Director.

'All sorts. Steel. Chemicals. Aviation. Leather. Footwear.'

'No oil?'

'We have a few petrochemical interests, but no oil as such.'

'Am I supposed to guess which conglomerate?'

'I think you know.'

'Wouldn't be the International Steel Consortium? Instecon?'

'Right first time . . .'

Alec looked around the bay; the sand was not overshadowed by buildings and thus got the sun all day. Several palm-frond shelters had been erected, with chairs and tables beneath them. What looked like a guest hut had been built in a stand of palms near the water's edge. An asphalt tennis court to the right, and the wooden structures of an outdoor gymnasium. Near by a channel had been excavated in the sand, and built up at the edges to form a natural diving stage for direct access to the sea; on the edge of the sand a swimming pool had been built, with diving boards, among low changing-rooms, and lounging seats all around its edge. A sailing dinghy had been dragged up on to the sand, and a flat sailing board which carried the single square sail and Jamaican rig. Out in the water, he could see the glisten of the buoys which doubtless kept the anti-shark net afloat beneath the surface. There was no sign of Veronica, the beauty queen – but hadn't Willie said she never exposed herself to the sun? In a country where all the visitors tanned an even golden brown, the sight of white flesh could perhaps

72

be stimulating. If you cared for that sort of sophistication, Alec thought.

'Great place, doncha think?' Sam said.

'Could become rather lonely . . .'

'You've come at a bad time. Last week at this time I could have offered you a choice of three broads . . .'

'I can take 'em or leave 'em,' Alec said. Don't push it; leave Sam make his own pace. Sam knows who you are, and why you're here. What he can't figure is how much you know about his intentions. Cat watches mouse, mouse watches cat. But who's the cat, and who the mouse? He could guess what was going through Sam's mind. What does this guy from Instecon want? Why has he come here? How much does he know? That would be the first series of thoughts. But then, behind them, would come the niggling suspicion, am I missing a play? Is there something I should know before I sell Instecon short? Have I underestimated them? Men like Sam Bantam couldn't afford to be seen to make a mistake with the market. Sam's reputation and his income depended on him being always right. If he recommended a sale of Instecon and the shares plummeted, his reputation would be riding high enough to carry him through any number of deals. If, on the other hand, he recommended selling, and the share price held, or what was worse increased before it held, his reputation could disappear overnight. Cat and mouse, but which is which?

'What brings you to the island?' Sam asked. 'Business or pleasure?'

'Both.'

'You keep a property here?'

'No, I stay in a hotel. The Casa Negra.'

'I've heard about that place. Looks kinda crummy, but it's said to be okay . . .'

'It suits me.'

'When'd you get here? With your kinda tan, it's hard to tell.'

'This morning.'

'The plane isn't in yet . . .'

'We have our own.'

'On the Delta, were you?'

'Yes.'

'Great plane . . .'

'We like it.'

'It's been worth a bundle to you, in the past . . .'

'It will continue to be worth what you call a bundle, in the future . . .'

'That's not exactly what I hear . . .'

Good, Alec thought. At last we've got some cards on the table. 'You don't strike me as the sort of man who believes all he hears.'

'I was christened with a pinch of salt,' Sam said.

Alec glanced at his watch. He had less than an hour. 'Do you read much, Mr Bantam?' he asked.

'Oh, for Christ's sake call me Sam, Alec.'

'Do you read much, Sam?'

'Sure, I read. Not much fiction though.'

'Company accounts?'

'Some, but not if they're fiction . . . Like you said earlier about broads, I can take 'em or leave 'em.'

'You ever seen the Instecon accounts, Sam?'

'You joking? I've seen the published versions . . . for the tourists and the penny ante investors.'

'I've got the house accounts in my bag . . .'

'You don't say. Certified?'

'You know we use Thornham Butcher, and Coal, Tarwick and Lambert.'

'Yeah, I had heard. These books, you running some kinda lending library?'

'Could be.'

'What's the subscription?'

'You'd need to give all your time to them, while you had them.'

'Like, no phone calls, uh?'

'That's right, no phone calls . . .' Alec said. He was enjoying the fencing, the thrust and parry. Each knew what the other was saying, but neither had committed himself. Alec would let Sam Bantam examine the house accounts of the Instecon Company, if Sam would not make his call to his New York brokers to instruct them to dispose of the Instecon shares. Alec knew the house accounts were impeccable; anyone capable of reading a balance sheet would see the madness of dumping two million shares on to the market at this time. But, just in case the ace was not enough this was the time to play the Joker.

'What's your prediction of the six-months value?' Alec asked Sam. It was an invitation to trade, and Sam knew it.

'What kind of volume?'

'Half a million shares . . .'

'*A* shares?'

Alec nodded.

Sam got up and walked round the veranda. Sometimes you arrange to buy shares in advance, and fix a price for them. In six months' time, that price could swing wildly in either direction. On the direction of that swing, a man could lose or win vast sums of money for himself. If he could take an option, say, on half a million shares at three hundred and five, and in six months' time those shares were worth three hundred and fifty-five, he'd have made a quarter of a million sterling. 'You might hold your own,' he said.

He sat down again. Alec looked him in the eye. The time for screwing around was past. 'I represent a consortium of Jacques de Blaie, Kenneth Severs, Sir Barton Underwood and myself,' he said.

'Your directors . . .'

'Yes, but in this matter we're acting in a private capacity. We are prepared to give you a six-months forward price for half a million shares of Instecon A at four hundred and eight.'

'Jesus Christ! Whatever the market price of Instecon A shares is in six months' time, you'll buy half a million off me at four hundred and eight . . .? You must be out of your minds. Anyway, I'm not holding a half million shares of Instecon A . . .'

'But we are. And we're prepared to agree to your purchasing them from us, in six months time, at today's market price, which I think you'll find will open at approximately three hundred and eight in New York in an hour's time.'

Sam Bantam chuckled, laughed, and then burst out in uncontrolled howling. He slapped his hand on the table, wiped the tears from his eyes. Alec Haig waited for him to calm down. 'You Limeys,' Sam Bantam said, between gulps, 'you slay me . . . Half a million pounds sterling, that's what you're offering me, in six months' time. But nothing crude, nothing phoney. I buy the shares from you, sell 'em back to you, and clear half a million for myself, and it never even costs me a cent. And just to make me rise to the hook, you bait it with your house accounts . . . Jesus Christ, Alec, I got to hand it to you, I really got to hand it to you.'

'Now if you don't mind,' Alec said, 'I think I'll have that cup of coffee . . .'

Sam Bantam invited Alec to swim in the bay, take out a boat, even move into the Frobisher Place for a day or two, but he politely refused. He left the accounts with Sam Bantam and was driven back to the Casa Negra, without once catching sight of the White Lady. Back at the Casa Negra he stripped again and walked along to the beach where he swam solidly for half an hour, trying to wash himself free of the hatred he had conceived for that coarse, fat, vulgar man. After his half-hour, he rented the water-ski boat with a driver, and they went whirling about the ocean off the town of Montego Bay, then back along the coast past the Frobisher Place. Several planes landed over his head while he was ski-ing; next year they'll all be Deltas, he thought with pride. When he returned, he showered and sat on his balcony, overlooking the ocean. Now the sun was blazing hot, and the balcony was filled with a searing light. Wearing only his shorts, Alec placed a call to New York, talked to Madonna for fifteen minutes, and to Ken. He dictated a tape that would be relayed to his office in Zürich, and contained enough work to keep his secretary there busy for a couple of days, and then put down the telephone. Now he could relax. He'd given Sam twenty-four hours to read the accounts, and would return to the Frobisher Place the following morning to get an answer on his deal for half a million shares. The profit Sam would make personally may have seemed a lot of money to anyone not thinking on the large scale, but Alec knew that Sam Bantam's support could be milked for every drop of its publicity value, and could reverse the trend out of the institutions, thus helping to maintain the share price, and even, over the next six months when the full value of the Vertical Take Off Lift plane became public knowledge, helping to advance the share price to more than the four hundred odd figure

Alec had predicted. In every sense the money they paid Sam Bantam would be well spent.

After a light lunch at the Casa Negra, Alec took a siesta in the heat of the afternoon. Gradually the beach had emptied itself as people came out of the blinding light and heat of the fierce midday sun. Occasionally, bright brittle laughter came from the bar at the end of the Casa Negra's terrace overlooking the water and the beach, but gradually that sound too died away, and calm descended on the hotel. Even the porter dozed in the doorway, his chin drooping to his chest.

They came at half past two, three of them. They wore ragged shorts, no shoes or shirts, and sun glasses. One of them was wearing a plaited-grass jipijapa hat. One by one they slipped past the slumbering doorman, and climbed the staircase to the first-floor rooms in the wing Alec occupied. They padded along the corridor to the end, climbed the barbed-wire obstacle and worked their way along the verandas, confident that anyone in the rooms would either be asleep or too occupied to see them. When they arrived at the veranda above the room next to the one in which Alec was sleeping they climbed over the edge by the grape-vine and dropped down on to the balcony below, silent as large cats. One of them padded to the screen which divided this room from Alec's. There was an eighteen-inch gap between the screen and the rail, narrow enough to maintain the idea of privacy, but wide enough not to impede anyone who wanted to build a better acquaintance with the person next door. He stood at the gap in the screen, listening. There was no sound from within the room. Sweat glistened on his black body. He had enormous shoulders and the flat stomach of an athlete, muscular thighs and hard bony legs and feet. He beckoned to the other two, similar in build, and they slipped through the gap one at a time, across the terrace, and into the outer

78

room. The door into the inner room was closed and the air conditioner was whirring, masking any slight shuffling sound they might make. The louvred shutters were closed to keep out the light. They stood together in an arrow-head wedge, and then went forward solid against the door. The flimsy lock burst open before their solid weight and then they were inside the room, in the fierce stab of light that had bounced in with them. Alec's eyes flashed open at the noise of the bursting door but the sudden light in the room blinded him momentarily, and as he blinked, the three men jumped across the room at him. Alec rolled by instinct and that saved him from the first of the blows, but as he went off the bed at the far side the kick the first man had aimed at him caught his kidneys and sent him crashing into the chest of drawers, gasping with pain. They leaped over the bed after him. Now Alec was fully awake. He chopped backwards with his hand and felt it connect in the crotch of the first assailant who went back grunting with pain. The second one kicked Alec on the side of his neck and head and Alec felt his ear tear under the blow but he caught hold of the man's foot in both hands, one behind the ankle, one across the toes and jerked savagely back and down, tearing the man's ankle muscles. The man tried to relieve the pressure by falling forward but Alec felt the muscle go, and knew the man wouldn't walk on that foot for quite a time. The third man had leapt off the bed and his feet were back and the bones of his knee-caps smashed into Alec's side, and Alec felt as if a ton weight had fallen on him and felt that at least one of his ribs must have cracked under the force of the weight of the Jamaican. He turned round and tried to struggle to his feet . . . anything to stop another of those pounding blows, but the man brought his knee forward again under Alec's chin and snapped his head back to smash again against the chest of drawers and Alec knew he would lose consciousness. He shot his arm out in desperation and felt it connect but he was too far gone to know where and on whom, and then he slumped down on the floor unconscious, aware only of a terrible fear, not that they would kill him, but that they would cripple him by kicking him in the terrible way he knew the Jamaicans fight, not with hand or fist, but with feet and knees and elbows, smashing bone beyond repair, maiming features beyond all recognition.

And so it would have been if Willie hadn't come along the corridor at that moment, heard the fighting inside, grabbed the mattock the gardeners had left at the base of a hibiscus in the garden outside Alec's door and used it to smash open the door. The three Jamaicans were a sorry sight. The first one who'd been smashed in the balls could hardly stand upright, the second whose ankle muscles had been torn was hobbling on one foot, and the third whose throat had been stabbed by Alec's last desperate straight arm blow into the windpipe was coughing and gasping for breath.

When the first blow came on the outside door they hobbled across the room, over the veranda, and flopped into the water twelve feet below. A fourth Jamaican had brought a glass-bottomed boat silently to the hotel. As they dived down he dragged them over the side of the boat, revved the engine and let in the clutch; the boat started to pull away with a plume of water and air scrabbling at its stern as it fought the inertia of the ocean. Several heads had appeared on several of the balconies when the smashing noise of Willie's mattock echoed through the rooms, and then Willie himself appeared on Alec's balcony, whirled the mattock, and let it fly after the departing boat. Its blade struck a terrifying thud into the back of the third Jamaican, the handle level with his shoulder blades, the other end of the blade protruding through the front of his body. He grunted and lifted his hands and clutched the end of the blade, then slumped down into the boat, blood gushing from his front and his back. The motor boat mounted speed as the blades gripped the water, and then it picked up and screamed out to sea. There were shouts from the other balconies when they saw the mattock blade hit the Jamaican's back, and the spurts of blood, but the screams ended abruptly when husbands drew their wives back into the rooms, fearful of becoming involved in what looked like a local fracas.

Willie wasted no more thought for the injured man; his body would be dumped overboard in shark-infested waters; he ran back into the room and lifted Alec Haig on to the bed, brought a towel soaked in cold water from the bathroom, and wiped Alec's skull below the lobe of his ear which had torn and was bleeding copiously. The telephone was ringing next to the bed; Willie took it from its cradle and left it to hang; he could hear the boys coming along the corridor outside knocking on doors, but he ignored them. The local police knew Willie, and he knew them, and everything could be explained later.

Alec Haig stirred on the bed; Willie wiped his face with the towel. Alec Haig's eyes opened. He saw Willie bending over him.

'Three men, Mr Haig, dey jump you . . .'

'I know. You recognize any of them?'

'Yes, Mr Haig, dey Kingston boys . . .'

'They get away?'

'All gone in a boat. But one of dem had a mattock sticking out of de back when last I see him . . .'

Alec looked up at Willie, then managed a half smile. 'Good man, Willie. You come and surprise 'em?'

'Yes, Mr Haig, I come along de corridor and hear de noise.

I break in de door and dey scuttle over de balcony into de water. Dey kicking you like you was a football.'

Alec felt a twinge of pain in his ribs. 'Like I was a football is right,' he said. 'Can you find me a doctor?'

'White man, or black man, Mr Haig?'

'No matter, so long as he's quick and efficient, and can keep his mouth closed.'

'Black man?'

'If you say so . . .'

Willie told the police they had seen and heard nothing, and the police knew better than to doubt him. He helped Alec out of the hotel and into the Lincoln. The black doctor lived in a house near the airport; he patched Alec's ear, strapped his broken rib, gave him a sedative, and told him to go back to bed and stay there for forty-eight hours. Alec gave the sedative pills to Willie, and got back into the car.

'One thing you forgot to tell me, Willie,' he said, as the car was driving down the road towards Montego Bay. 'How did you happen to come walking along the corridor at that particular moment? You knew I wouldn't need you until this evening . . .?'

Willie slapped his forehead. 'My God and dammit,' he said, 'I dey forget all about it. I dey come to tell you, Mr Sam Bantam and de White Lady done leave de Frobisher Place, and gone to Mr Bantam's boat.'

'Get me down to the wharf as quick as you can.'

Willie put his foot down, drove through the resort section of the outskirts of Montego Bay like a wild wind.

But when they reached the wharf by the yacht club, the *Liberty Belle* had sailed on the afternoon tide, tanks and food lockers full, destination unknown.

When Alec returned to the Casa Negra, a portfolio of papers was waiting for him. The portfolio contained the company accounts, and a note from Sam Bantam. 'An interesting proposition. We must talk about it sometime.'

Alec Haig ordered the Delta pilot to prepare for immediate take-off, then phoned New York. The share price of Instecon International had dropped to two hundred and seventy point four five, the lowest it had been for two years. And, Madonna told him, it was still falling.

Sam Bantam had sold out.

PHASE 6

The Italian International Airlines flight 775 for London was due to leave da Vinci Airport at 1900 hours. The plane had been serviced that morning under Instecon supervision and had stood in the Italian Airlines hangar all day. At 1645 it was tractored out on to the apron, and Willie Smedhurst left the Instecon office to go to the plane to make his pre-flight check. He was carrying a clipboard and a pen as he made his way through the passenger terminal; he stopped at the cigarette shop to buy a packet of Nazionale cigarettes and a box of waxed matches, then made his way through the side door marked 'staff only' and across the restricted area of the tarmac to where the Italian Airlines Delta was waiting. The plane was already fuelled and ready, should he pass it, to take its place on the departure apron. As he drew near the plane he looked around him, but could see no sign of Giuseppi Faolli, the engineer who was supposed to make the check with him. He clucked angrily, climbed the passenger ramp, and went into the cockpit, hoping to find Faolli there. He sat in the skipper's seat, waited for five minutes then, still angry, he took his clipboard and nodded to the guard looking up at him to warn him to keep the area clear, since Willie was about to start the engines. He swore when he saw he must have dropped the pen out of his clip-board, cursed when he tapped his pockets and realized he hadn't another.

'Damn Faolli,' he said. If nothing else, Faolli would have

been carrying a pen with him. He could make the check single handed, but Instecon regulations specified that two men should be present, and Willie had a healthy respect for order and regulations. He'd damned well told Faolli he'd do the check at 1645, and by now Faolli ought to have known him well enough to realize Willie was a stickler for doing things correctly, and on time. He glanced around the cockpit, was suddenly relieved when he saw a ballpoint pencil had been left on the fascia to the right of his hand. It was an Italian International Airlines publicity pencil, the sort they hand out to passengers. Inside the body of the pencil was a liquid which drained down as you tipped the pencil, revealing the logo and the name of the airline. He entered his name on the head of the report, and filled in the date and the time, the flight number, the airline, and the code letter of the aircraft.

Damn Faolli; he wouldn't wait. His decision to go ahead alone with the test wasn't in keeping with company regulations but, he asked himself, which would be better, to carry out the test on his own or make no test and ground the plane. Then there'd be hell to pay, wouldn't there?

His decision made, he set the computer programmer to 'engine start', switched the button, and waited. Within seconds the first engine fired, and the test began.

Forty-five minutes later Giuseppi hadn't arrived and Willie had put the last tick on the last page of the check list. He climbed out of the airplane, nodded to the guard on duty, locked the black box into its compartment in the fuselage of the plane after setting it, and made his way to the engineer's quarters to look for the Italian.

Giuseppi was nowhere to be found.

Willie took his report to the office of the Chief Engineer of Italian International Airlines, and handed it over, with his

85

written authorization for the plane to fly and the Instecon 'fit for service' guarantee.

On his way back to the Instecon office, he looked into the terminal to see if he could find Giuseppi. A man standing by the coffee bar looked vaguely familiar to him, but there was no sign of Giuseppi. When Willie got back to the Instecon Engineer's office, he made a notation on the day pad to inform them that Giuseppi Faolli had neglected to turn up for duty, then left the office for the day. On his way to pick up his car he saw again the man he thought he'd recognized inside the terminal; something was vaguely familiar about him, but Willie couldn't say what, and started to drive back to Rome. He was sweating profusely, and promised himself a shower the moment he arrived home.

From the seat of his parked Fiat, Giuseppi Faolli watched Willie Smedhurst leave the airport. Great. Great. If Willie had stayed at the airport at the end of his shift, Faolli had instructions to call a number in Rome; but Willie had left normally, and now Giuseppi could drive into Rome and collect the *lire* he'd been promised.

Crazy, wasn't it? But who was he to argue?

And all so secret. Jesus, they must be loaded!

He'd done as he'd been told, booked a room at the Paragon under the name of João Gilberto from Rio de Janeiro. He'd had to fake up his accent a bit, but the man on the desk hadn't made any comment. That Paragon on the Via Veneto! Some place, hey? And what a great room, the best room he'd ever been in. Felt just simply great, walking into the Paragon, just like one of the rich *Americani*, and taking the room that had been booked for him by phone. Paid for the room in cash, too. And a few *lire* to buy a drink in the bar.

He arrived at the Paragon, went up to his room, stretched out on the bed, picked up the bedside phone.

'Give me Mr Copeland's suite,' he said, and was connected almost instantly. 'Mr Copeland? Mr Gilberto here, you know, from Rio de Janeiro.'

Mr Copeland came straight up. Damn good of him, he brought a cup of coffee with him.

'How did everything go?' he asked.

'Fine, just fine, like you said. Seems a hell of an elaborate way to play a birthday joke on a man. Must be costing you a fortune, with what you're paying for this room, and what you're paying me ...'

'Don't you worry about what it's costing,' Mr Copeland said, 'just drink your coffee ...'

*　　　*　　　*

Flight 775 from Rome to London was fully booked, half the seats being occupied by a Catholic organization which took thousands of children annually to the Vatican on a two-nights-and-three-days pilgrimage. The party was in the charge of a layman tour director with three priests and three nuns to help him. The flight was called thirty minutes before take-off time, Gate Eight, and the schoolchildren marched in crocodile through Immigration and Customs, across and along the departure hall, out on to the tarmac, and on to the plane. Loaded in good time, the plane door was sealed, the skipper asked for and received tower clearance and taxied out to the end of the runway for take-off.

This was only the third flight Arnaldo Semprevoni had made as skipper of a Delta but he was not the sort to be nervous. He had confidence in himself, the airline, and the aircraft, a good crew in the cockpit and back in the cabin. He'd be sleeping in London that night with Annunciata, the second stewardess, and she had a body of a shape most men can only imagine in dreams. The plane responded perfectly on take-off under his hands, equally skilled at lifting a plane or a woman into the clouds. They reached thirty-five thousand feet in good time while the coast of Italy was still visible; the radio operator gave them the check from the Pisa beacon, and the Nice beacon lay straight ahead and its signal would be received in a minute or so at the speed at which they were travelling. The computer, programmed for the London run, would automatically pick up each landmark as they came to it or buzz a warning and print out the emergency action should the beacon fail to appear on schedule.

Three things happened only two of which were known to Arnaldo Semprevoni. Immediately after take-off, the layman tour operator groaned and slumped in his seat. Annunciata bent over him and recognized by his heavy breathing, heightened colour, gasping pain-raddled breath, that she had a medical emergency on her hands. Calmly she walked to her station at the back of the plane and made a brief announcement. 'If there is a doctor on the plane would he please press his call button.' A light immediately came on two seats behind that occupied by the tour director. She hurried forward and took the doctor with her to the sick man. He made a brief investigation, but already his skilled diagnostic eye had told him what was wrong.

He whispered to Annunciata. 'Appendix,' he said. 'We

must get this man down on the ground just as soon as possible.'

Annunciata left the doctor with the sick man and hurried forward into the cabin. Using the internal telephone, quickly she told Arnaldo Semprevoni what the doctor had said.

That was the first thing that happened.

At that moment the computer began a print-out. The radio operator read it, pressed the button to put it on the closed circuit television screen to the co-pilot. The message read, 'Fog Warning at L.A.P. Minimum holding thirty minutes. Alternates Shannon, Paris, Glasgow, Amsterdam.'

The co-pilot switched his intercom to the skipper, and repeated the computer print-out.

So far as the skipper was concerned, that was the second thing that happened. The second emergency of which he was aware. He nodded to the co-pilot, nodded to Annunciata, switched his intercom to the radio operator. 'Get me clearance for an emergency landing in Nice,' he said. The co-pilot heard what he said, and while the radio operator was calling the tower at Nice Airport, the co-pilot switched on the landing instructions screen, which showed a picture of the information he and the pilot would need to know to get into Nice Airport. He then switched the computer to 'land' and the computer took over all the details of losing speed and height to prepare the aircraft for its descent to the ground. The radio operator pressed his 'okay to land' button, and the co-pilot pointed it out to Arnaldo, who, however, had already seen it.

Now the skipper himself talked to the tower at Nice Airport, requesting an ambulance, and possible emergency procedures for an acute appendix case. The professional part of his mind was cool as ice, each action performed with absolute precision. This was his job, and he was good at it. Of course the Delta plane itself helped with its sophisticated system of intercommunication, its computer brain that would fly the aircraft to any destination and, if necessary, land it without human agency, once it was appropriately switched. So sophisticated was the system that, when necessary, the switching could be carried on from the ground. The fog alert over London hadn't worried Arnaldo; the Delta could be landed in zero visibility. The plane came into Nice and went straight on the beam for a first-time landing. Arnaldo took the controls himself and set the plane on the runway without even a bump. No matter how good a computer landing may be it doesn't have the finesse of an experienced man's hands on the controls, feeling the motion of the plane even at that high landing speed, easing it down feather light on to the runway. Working together as one. Arnaldo and the co-pilot went through the slowing, braking and taxi-ing procedures that put the plane exactly where the tower had instructed, near the perimeter fence with easy access for the passenger disembarkation steps, and the waiting ambulance.

From the time the doctor asked Annunciata to get the patient back on the ground as quickly as possible, to the time the patient was placed inside an ambulance to scream off to the nearest hospital with sirens blowing and lights flashing, only five minutes and fifteen seconds had elapsed. The Delta door was closed again and pressurization began after only eight minutes had elapsed. Arnaldo requested clearance from the tower and was directed to proceed to the end of the runway for immediate take-off. He arrived in position after an elapsed seventeen minutes.

'Not bad going, eh?' the co-pilot said, 'we got that man down on the ground and we'll arrive on time in London.' Arnaldo smiled at the co-pilot, gave him a thumbs-up sign. Elapsed time, seventeen minutes and fifteen seconds.

Arnaldo adjusted the ear-piece of his radio headset,

wondering what was taking the tower so long to give him clearance for take-off. He was at the end of the runway in position and the previous plane had taken off two minutes ago. Seventeen minutes and twenty-five seconds.

Then, one by one, three red lights were illuminated on the panel, part of the complex of dials and lights and switches and indicators with which the cockpit was festooned, if such a word could be applied to engineering precision.

The first red light indicated the main electrical supply system had failed and the emergency electric supply system had taken over.

The second red light indicated the emergency electric supply system had failed and the second emergency system had taken over.

But the third red light told them all electric supply systems, main, replacement, and emergencies, had failed and other than the small battery which served the panel lights, the Delta was now without electric power.

The engines stopped.

'Sacred Mother,' Arnaldo said, as hurriedly he crossed himself. 'If that had happened when we were racing down the runway for take-off. Or when we were thirty thousand feet up . . .'

The co-pilot couldn't hear him. The radio was dead.

The plane had been crippled.

*   *   *

Alec Haig was about to take off from Jamaica when the news was received of the grounding of the plane at Nice. Alec changed his flight plan and arrived at Nice Airport at midnight. The plane had been tractored into a service hangar, and the passengers had already left for London.

The tour director, despite the speed of the emergency help he had received, had died in Nice Hospital of a burst appendix. Once he'd lost consciousness on the plane, he'd never recovered it. A couple of the nuns reported he'd complained to them, during the tour, of pains in his stomach which he'd put down to changes of food. Alec had ordered by radio telephone that the staff engineers who'd certified the plane be flown to Nice to be there when Alec arrived. Alec had a hundred questions to ask them.

By the time Alec landed, they had found the fault. A bi-metal strip, which served the function of emergency cut-out and regulator, had been installed the wrong way round. As a result a servo pipe had overheated and had fractured. The engineer estimated it would take about twenty minutes for the servo fluid to drain through the fracture; when that happened the servo-operated solenoids in the fuel-feed regulating system would jam, and the electrics would overheat. Normally the bi-metallic strip would then open further to bring in the emergency cooling system, but since the bi-metal was installed the wrong way round, any excess of heat only closed it more tightly instead of opening it. Result, electric burn-out on all systems, including the generators.

Alec climbed into the cockpit. Jules Charrier, the chief Instecon engineer at Nice, had taken the cover from the panel that contained the bi-metallic strip, but had not removed the strip until Alec could see it for himself. Alec looked silently at it. Willie Smedhurst from Rome had climbed aboard with him, and Alec gestured at the panel containing the strip. Willie looked aghast at it. An emergency electric supply had been plugged into the plane, and Alec reached across Jules to the dashboard panel and depressed a switch. A light glowed on a dial above the switch, and the needle rapidly climbed the face of the dial to a position marked overload. When the needle reached overload, the light began to wink on and off. Willie had brought his copy of the pre-flight check report with him from Rome. He opened it at page six. Pressing that switch, as Alec Haig had just done, was part of the check that he had carried out. There was a tick in the box which referred to that particular test, that specific switch.

'I just don't believe it,' he said, his voice trembling with uncertainty. 'That bi-metal must have been changed round after I did the check.'

He looked at Alec and at Jules. All three of them knew that what he was suggesting was impossible. To break down that panel, take out the bi-metal and put it back in the wrong way round would take at least two and a half hours.

'What time did you finish your check?' Alec asked.

The time had been entered on the pad, plain for all to see.

Alec pointed to the pilot's log, printed out by the computer. The flight had been airborne at 1859 hours, less than two hours after the check was completed. 'Could you strip all that down, replace the bi-metal and put it all back together again in under two hours?' Alec asked Jules, but each already knew the answer.

They left the plane in the hands of the mechanics who'd replace the faulty servo system and the bi-metal panel, who'd check every speck of that plane with microscopic care before putting it back in service. Alec and Willie Smedhurst went into the Instecon office, Willie feeling as if he were going to the guillotine. Jules had given them the use of his quarters. Alec sat in one of the two chairs on the near side of the desk, and Willie nervously sat on the edge of the other.

'What happened, Willie?' Alec asked.

Willie shook his head. 'I don't know, Mr Haig,' he said. 'I can't think of anything . . .'

'Right, let's take it step by step. In chronological order. Did you drink or eat with anybody before the flight check?'

'Nobody, Mr Haig, I swear it. Do you think I'd be foolish enough to take such a risk after what happened to Ross Compton. Since you sent round that confidential internal memo, not one of us will take the risk of drinking anything with anybody before we make a flight check. I didn't take a single drink, or eat a single bite after my lunch, and that I prepared myself in my own flat in Rome this morning before I drove out to the airport on duty. A half bottle of Valpolicella, a salad, a piece of bread, and a hunk of *provolone*. It was all locked in my briefcase, which was never out of my sight except when it was locked away in my desk in the Instecon building.'

'All right, Willie. Don't misunderstand me. You're not in doubt, I don't have any suspicions about you, believe me. Now, what happened to Faolli?'

'I don't know, Mr Haig, I truly don't know. He's not a bad kid. A bit lazy maybe, but that's the only criticism I might have. He's never been late before, never failed to turn up for a pre-flight check. I've back-tracked and so far as the office knows, he left them in plenty of time to meet me at the plane. Now we can't find him. We've telephoned all over Rome, and we can't find him anywhere.'

'Did you see him at all today?'

'Yes. We checked out the India Airways flight together. Of course the first thing I did when I heard about this was to check that flight again, but they've arrived all right on the ground in Delhi.'

'All right. Now, the check itself. Can you think of anything unusual about it? What, for example, was the oil pressure on the starboard link connector . . .?'

'Page four, eh. I've got that ticked.'

'I know you've ticked it, Willie, but you must have read that figure. What was it?'

Willie scratched his head, chewed the end of the pencil he'd picked up with the clip board. 'It was . . . well, I can't exactly remember what it was but it must have been all right, mustn't it, or I wouldn't have ticked it . . .?'

'The bi-metal wasn't all right, and yet you ticked that, Willie . . .'

Willie flushed with anger. 'Look here, Mr Haig, I've worked for Instecon now for five years and . . .'

'Nobody's questioning your loyalty, Willie, but it's a certain fact that, if the tour director hadn't suffered a burst appendix, everyone aboard that plane would have been dead now, and Instecon would have lost a Delta in one of the worst air disasters ever known.'

'Then what's the answer, Mr Haig? I know damned well I put a tick on that page, and I know equally well I wouldn't have ticked that item if that warning light had been blinking at me . . .'

'. . . if you had been *aware* that the warning light was blinking at you . . . Okay, Willie, let's start again at the beginning. Tell me everything you can remember doing today from the time you got out of bed.'

The interrogation lasted well over four hours and by that time Willie was dropping with exhaustion, his mood varying between anger at some of the questions Alec asked over and over again, and terrible guilt feelings that perhaps he might have been responsible for an act of negligence that could have caused the deaths of all those people and the loss of a plane. After two hours Alec had established a pattern, and knew the drug Professor Baxter had identified for him had been used again. Willie had suffered a specific loss of memory in the middle of the pre-flight check; shortly afterwards he had sweated profusely. But how the devil had the drug been administered, and by whom?

*   *   *

The emergency switchboard operator in Zürich found Alec in Nice and plugged through the call from Kwam T'ang in Hong Kong. Kwam T'ang didn't like using the telephone; the payment you got for the information you conveyed could never be held in your hand while you were talking. Not that Kwam T'ang had any reason to doubt Mr Haig, but many generations of cautious Chinese had gone into his making.

'You have a price for my shares, Kwam T'ang?' Alec asked, cutting short the endless Oriental courtesies.

'I have information, Mr Haig, if you can hear me when I speak.'

'I can hear you, Kwam T'ang, as plainly as you can hear me. Now what sort of information do you have?'

'Valuable information, Mr Haig, one might almost say priceless information, Mr Haig.'

'I'll give you a thousand dollars. Not a penny more. And let me warn you, Kwam T'ang, I don't have time for trading . . .'

He heard the gasp on the other end of the telephone. In Kwam T'ang's philosophy, a man who had no time for trading had no time for life. 'Now, tell me, do you have a price for my shares?'

He heard Kwam T'ang chuckle. 'Very good, Mr Haig.

One thousand dollars American, agreed. In cash. Any time to suit yourself. That's your side of the bargain. Now my side is as follows. No, I have not been able to obtain a price for your shares. Not to sell them in strength, bound together as the branches of a tree. But I do have this piece of information. Certain friends of mine have been informed that to buy Instecon International shares at this time would be very foolish, since very quickly those shares will be worth no more than the paper from which people build houses. If I were a fanciful man I would say the cold winds from the mountains are blowing across your rich fields, and soon your crop will fail like stricken rice . . .'

'Why is the share price going to fail, Kwam T'ang?'

'Because the Delta aeroplane on which your fortunes at present are founded is not a good aeroplane, Mr Haig, or so my informant tells me, and soon your aeroplane is going to fall out of the sky like a tattered kite, and with it will fall the fortunes of those people foolish enough to invest their money in your company . . .'

Kwam T'ang chuckled at the other end of the line. His vast wealth was in land and buildings, gold and silver and diamonds, and watching the rise and fall of share prices was a foolish game for immature, unlearned westerners and grasping Nipponese.

Alec kept his voice calm, almost icy. 'And who is the source of this wisdom, Kwam T'ang? Which washerwoman had chattered this "knowledge" to your servants . . .?'

Kwam T'ang chuckled again. 'He who rises to provocation already commits one indiscretion, Mr Haig. Of course no washerwoman told my servants this knowledge, but since you have agreed to pay me a thousand dollars, a sum of money almost without value for such a priceless gem, I will reveal the source of my knowledge, if not of my information.

Many men do not like your Delta airplane, Mr Haig. Doubtless they believe it to be as good as any airplane can be, without considering the folly of men who imitate birds and try to fly round the Heavens. But the Delta airplane, it would seem, is stealing the markets of airplanes in which they have money invested, and these men wish to do your airplane a harm. I understand that a meeting took place recently at which the leader of these men was able to say that your airplane is not a good one. He was able to produce to this meeting a confidential document which suggested that the maintenance on your plane was not of the best. The men present at that meeting were all important financial people and they were most impressed by the evidence. Since the meeting was held in such secrecy, however, it was agreed between them that the matter would be kept hidden, until such time as they had sold their shares for the maximum value they could obtain. If you look at what has happened to your share price, it would seem that they have all sold out now . . .'

'Where was this meeting held, Kwam T'ang?'

'I understand it was held in an island of the Caribbean, in a house known as the Frobisher Place. And the name of the man who held the meeting . . .'

'Is Mr Sam Bantam, Kwam T'ang.'

PHASE 7

Sally Michaels had formerly been employed in the South Wales Instecon steel plant; now she was Alec Haig's private secretary and worked mainly in Zürich. When first employed by him, she had accompanied him on his many journeys about the world, but no girl can take easily to living out of a suitcase, as Alec himself could, and Sally had established a network of secretaries who could look after his day-to-day routines in any of the larger Instecon offices, with instant communication to Zürich as required.

It was Sally who had conceived and organized the service by which anybody in a 'sensitive' post could communicate with Alec Haig, day or night, anywhere he might be merely by picking up a company telephone and dialling a certain code. Those lines were used only in emergency. Sally herself, however, had no need to use the service when she wanted to talk to Alec Haig on the morning after he had been interrogating Willie Smedhurst, since she herself had made the booking for him in the Grand Hotel, Nice.

She heard the *brr-brr* as the hotel operator tried his room, then the click as the telephone was lifted, and Alec's still sleepy voice.

'When are you coming back to Zürich?' she asked, without need to identify herself.

'I'm not sure. I may still have things to do here.'

'What things? I've had Willie Smedhurst flown here; the engineer's report is on my desk, and the plane is ready to fly as soon as you give the okay. They'll be bringing you a copy of the report when they bring your breakfast, which should be in five minutes. I've ordered corn flakes, yoghourt, and bacon on toast the way you like it. And coffee. The car will be outside the hotel at half past nine and your plane takes off at half past ten . . .'

'I want them to check the Company plane before it flies . . .'

'They're doing that right now . . . I've booked you with Francair Charter . . .'

There was a pause. 'Something behind all this, Sally,' he said. 'I'm used to your super-efficiency by now but I get a feeling you want me back in Zürich in a hurry, and you're not telling me the real reason . . .'

'You're dead right,' she said laughing, 'I want you back in Zürich before you go flying off to New York or London, or Hong Kong, or Jamaica again . . .'

'What's the reason, Sally? Or can't you say on the telephone?'

'You are a nincompoop,' she said, drawing out the vowel sounds in her sing-song voice which never seemed to lose its Welsh accent. 'Have you forgotten what today is?'

'The board meeting? I thought that was tomorrow?'

'It's not the board meeting . . .'

'The day for signing my expense account . . .?'

'It's not the day for signing your expense account . . .'

'Okay, Sally, I'm awake now, and I'm a big boy, so you can tell me in plain words of one syllable . . .'

'We have a date tonight, Alec,' she said softly, 'though I imagine you've forgotten. It's your birthday. Many happy returns.'

100

There were flowers on his breakfast tray when the waiter brought it in.

*   *   *

When Alec arrived in Zürich it was decided to hold the board meeting rather than wait until the following day. Four worried directors sat around the table in Sir Barton Underwood's office; their gloom increased when Kenneth Severs gave them the latest stock market quotation.

'We're still buying?' Sir Barton asked. Kenneth Severs nodded. As fast as the shares came on the market, they bought them in at the asking price, rather than let the shares sink to a panic level. But they couldn't go on buying indefinitely, and already each of them had underwritten bank loans that began to have the proportions of a National Debt.

'And the institutions are still selling?' Again Kenneth Severs nodded. 'It's up to Jacques and Alec now,' he said.

Alec briefly outlined what he had found out, what he had guessed, what he knew and thought. As usual he named no names. Sir Barton never wanted to know the details of Alec's activities. 'A group of men heavily involved in the aerospace industry and losing money rapidly because of the success of the Delta, is trying to get back at us. They've started a rumour campaign that the Delta is a bad piece of machinery and that we're likely to have a crash with it any day due to a design fault. They held a secret meeting in Montego Bay, and invited top financial advisers from the big institutions. At that meeting they produced evidence – well, what they call evidence – that we were cheating on maintenance.'

'Dammit, that accounts for something that's been puzzling

me,' Sir Barton said. 'I met Sir Montague Weinschraub in the club the other day. Can't stand the fellow, but we've always been on howd'ye do terms. Weinschraub and Solomon act for International Insurance of London, as you all doubtless know. The damn fellow cut me dead. Cut me, in the club. Now I know why. He thought we were taking 'em for a ride when we recommended Instecon International . . .'

'Why wasn't George Phillimore invited to Jamaica?' Kenneth Severs asked, puzzled.

'Because they know we use Phillimore sometimes. They've been very clever. They only invited people who don't act for us; that was the only way they could keep it absolutely dead secret. That's why we haven't even heard a rumour until this late stage.'

'If that's all it is,' Jacques said, 'we can just sit back and wait until the rumours die down. That sort of tongue-wagging never did anyone any harm in the long run.'

'I'm afraid there's more to it,' Alec said. 'They must have got to some members of our staff. I don't know which ones, yet, and I don't know how many, but believe me I'll find out. So far the score is one man dead, though legally he's counted as a natural death, and two men missing, one in London and one in Rome. The group is taking active steps to crash one of our Deltas . . .'

'Oh my God,' Sir Barton said, his face blanching. 'Do you think they'll manage it?'

'I don't think so. I know what method they are using, and I'm certain I can counteract it.'

'But are you absolutely positive, Alec? If not, we have no alternative but to ground all Deltas immediately. We must not run the risk of any aeroplane flying if madmen are trying to crash it. And what's more, we must inform the police at once.'

'Then everyone will say it's true what the rumours imply that the Delta is a bad aircraft,' Jacques said.

'It would force our shares down to the very bottom,' Kenneth Severs added. 'And it would give us a cash-flow problem since our credit ratings are linked to our share price.'

'Look here, I don't give a damn about the shares,' Sir Barton said, as angry as anyone had ever seen him. 'I'm not thinking about cash flow . . . My sole concern is for the lives of innocent passengers who entrust themselves to our aeroplane. If there's any danger at all . . .'

'I truly think I have them licked, Sir Barton,' Alec said, but Sir Barton looked gravely at him. Modern business methods often didn't bear analysis and Alec Haig had done many things Sir Barton really would rather not know; but now that the lives of innocent people were at stake, he knew he could no longer stand aloof. 'You'd better tell me what this one is all about, Alec,' he said. Alec told them everything, starting with the suspicions and the death of Ross Compton, the findings of Professor Baxter, the attempt on his own life in Jamaica, Willie Smedhurst's loss of memory, the sabotage to the Delta which, mercifully, had landed in Nice.

When he heard about the bi-metal, Sir Barton shook his head. 'And half the passengers on that flight were children?' he said. Alec nodded. Sir Barton looked around the table.

'Gentlemen,' he said, 'I think we have reached the end of the road. I don't see how we can continue. Certainly I cannot continue to sit in this chair, knowing I am placing the life of one of my fellow directors in constant jeopardy, and that innocent people may be killed for no better reason than that they chose to fly in one of our planes.'

'What is the alternative, Sir Barton? I knew what I was doing when I took on this job. I accept the dangers, just as I accept the financial rewards and the free-wheeling life. But I

103

hate thieves and anybody who stoops low to fight us because they don't have better products and better management.'

'All right, Alec. I accept that you are a volunteer and that you have the right to weigh the rewards against the dangers and make up your own mind. But the passengers, Alec, are the ones I'm thinking about, caught in the middle of this terrible affair. Rather than risk one life, I'd put the whole of Instecon into liquidation immediately.'

Sir Barton was a decent man, involved in the wheels of big business. He was a brilliant man and of course ruthless in business. But behind his impressive Captain of Industry façade he still retained a human and susceptible conscience. They all argued across the board table for two hours, but Sir Barton could not be shaken. No Delta could fly until the threat to passengers' lives had been ended.

Alec Haig and Jacques de Blaie were able to wring one concession from him. Jacques could mount a public relations flight. On it would be invited VIPs and press men only. Alec personally would check the pre-flight maintenance, with a suitably qualified engineer. Only if Alec were absolutely certain the plane had not been interfered with would the plane take off. The plane would fly to Montego Bay in Jamaica with its public relations guests and then would return to England. After that, no more Deltas would fly until it was demonstrably obvious that the group of men led by Sam Bantam had been utterly destroyed.

Each of them knew that in making his decision and sticking to it, Sir Barton was putting his entire fortune at risk. If the Instecon company crashed, Sir Barton would be penniless.

*   *   *

The board meeting had just ended when Alec took the call from Willie in Jamaica.

'Your friend dey come back, and de White Lady.'

'Where had he been?'

'De coastguard say your friend been fishing to de Caymans; but he doant't bring back no fish.'

'Any news of my visitors . . .'

'One of de visitors is missing. De others dey hiding in a village outside Kingston, and dey sorry sorry men.'

'Can you get someone to keep an eye on them for me?'

'I do better dan dat, Mr Haig. I teach 'em a lesson, no fear, dey not do dat again when Willie finish with dem.'

'No lessons, Willie,' Alec said. 'They were paid to do a job, and I have no hard feelings.'

'Mr Haig, you amaze me,' Willie said. Eye for an eye, tooth for a tooth, has been the recourse of primitive men throughout all time. Willie was affronted to think of thugs getting away without punishment.

'That's in the past, Willie. Now I'm interested in the future. You said something about a house-boy being interested in a certain lady . . .'

'Interested not de word, Mr Haig.'

'You know the house-boy?'

'I know everybody, Mr Haig.' It was not a boast; Willie truly had an encyclopaedic knowledge of what went on in Jamaica.

'Would he work for us?'

'If de wages good, de fella work for anybody. He interested in only one thing, de devil money . . .'

'But he's interested in the girl?'

'Only for de devil money, Mr Haig.'

Alec Haig thought for a moment, his distaste aroused by the thought of using this Jamaican house-boy who'd do anything for money. It's doubtful Alec would have used him, if the Board of Instecon hadn't just grounded the Delta fleet.

'I'm sending two friends to Jamaica, Willie. A Mr Pappa-yanakis and a Mr Giovanni. They'll make contact with you when they arrive; look after them for me. And make certain they don't have any visitors like the ones I had, understood?'

'Understood, Mr Haig.'

*   *   *

Willie Smedhurst was in the hands of an industrial psychologist from Vienna, and a consultant psychiatrist from Munich. Willie Smedhurst was being made to re-live every second of the previous day, every thought, every feeling, every sensation, every memory. His entire life, for one day, was being mapped with the careful precision of a bank-note etching. Not only what he did, but when, where, how and, most important, why. It was a long, slow and wearying process, but the dark recesses of Willie's mind were being turned inside out.

*   *   *

Immediately after the board meeting Alec Haig called a press conference. Only the agencies were invited, no aviation correspondents, no TV men, no newspapers. The press conference was held in his own office; five agency men, Alec Haig and his personal assistant Hank Dawson. Hank gave each of the press men a drink, greeting them all personally, then perched himself on the edge of the desk behind which Alec was already sitting. 'I'll go through the ground rules,' he said informally. 'We have a statement for you which Mr Haig will read . . .'

'So hand it to us, Hank; we can read,' Arthur Verries said good-naturedly.

'No, I don't think we'll do that,' Hank said.

'You could have put it in the post, or sent it round by messenger . . .'

'And done us out of a drink . . .?' Tom Halliburton said.

'You'll also notice when you get the folders that we've omitted the usual two-hundred-page review of the company's activities, the free ballpoint pen, the gold tie-clip with the Instecon insignia . . .'

'Too bad,' John Casserotto said, 'I've forgotten to bring a pen with me since you always hand 'em out.'

Hank picked up a pen from Alec's desk, and threw it towards John. All of them knew this was a settling down process. They knew that, since Alec Haig, a director of Instecon, was going to read a statement, the occasion was an important one, and anything said could be attributed directly. No 'it-was-reliably-reported-that . . .' stories which journalists detest as much as readers and viewers. 'Mr Haig will read a prepared statement, and you'll be given a transcript. Then we'll talk about it.' He pressed the intercom key on Alec's desk and Sally came in with folders. He piled the folders on the desk, and waited until Sally had left.

Alec took a folder, opened it, extracted the top page, and began to read. His voice was cold and unemotional.

'The many airlines who use the Delta plane
manufactured by our company Instecon
Aviation have today been informed that,
effective immediately, all Delta aircraft
in airline service have been grounded.'

'My God,' Don Berrimore said. 'One of 'em crashed . . .?'

'It wasn't on our wire,' John Casserotto said, looking around at his colleagues.

'If Mr Haig could continue, gentlemen,' Hank said impatiently, 'the statement is not yet finished.'

> 'In its constant search for improvements,
> our aviation engineer research department
> has developed a modification to the tailplane
> assembly which will add in-flight stability,
> and our company believes it should pass on
> the benefits of that research immediately.'

'God damn it, I know one of 'em's crashed,' Don Berrimore said. 'What's all this crap about tailplanes . . .'

Despite the interruption, Alec continued to speak.

> 'Instecon Aviation is co-operating with
> each airline to ensure no scheduled flights
> will be delayed or cancelled, and any
> inconvenience caused to passengers is kept
> to an absolute minimum.'

He stopped speaking. The agency men looked at each other, stunned. 'If I file a statement like that,' Don Berrimore said, 'London will dig out my pension book . . .'

John Casserotto read through his notes. 'You want us to believe this load of bullshit, Mr Haig? For Christ's sake come off it. The Delta fleet's grounded and all you can give us is fifteen lousy lines. What's happened? Has a Delta plane crashed? Yes or no?'

'This statement has nothing to do with a Delta plane having crashed . . .' Hank Dawson said.

'So what about the Delta that made an unscheduled stop at Nice? We filed a story, which you put out from this very office, that the plane had come down because a passenger was suffering a burst appendix. You got a lot of good human interest publicity out of me for that story, Hank, damn it. I filed three books on "the Company that wasn't too big to care . . . " Don't tell me it was a phoney . . .?'

Hank shook his head, turned, and appealed to Alec Haig who put up his hand to quieten the news man. 'Listen to me, fellows,' he said, 'and let's get one thing quite straight. This office never has and never will put out a phoney story. We gave you the Nice story absolutely straight. I give you my word of honour that the sole reason for that unscheduled touch-down in Nice, the sole reason, was because of that man's appendix.'

'So what's with this crap about grounding the fleet? Come on, Mr Haig, New York will piss 'emselves laughing if I file it the way you've given it to us. Look, I know we've had a lot of junkets out of Instecon, and a helluva lot of hospitality, but we've accepted only because you've always come up with a story we can use. You've never gone in for puffs. But this is too much! Or should I say too little? It's as much as my job's worth to file the statement you've just read out without some kind of a backgrounder. Christ, when that story gets on the wire and there's no follow-up, you'll have every newspaper in the world writing gossip column crap . . .'

'Did you hope to lose it on page nine?' Don said. 'We've seen what's happening to your share price the last few hours. This story'll make every front page in the world. And the aviation features, and the finance pages, and the gossips and diaries. You must know that!'

Alec rose to his feet. 'Hank and I are going to take a short walk down the corridor,' he said. 'While we're gone, chew it over, take a drink, help yourselves to a cigarette. But I can tell you this much, when I get back, any question you might ask me will get a no-comment, if it has anything to do with that statement I've just made.'

He and Hank went out together. The agency men sat there, looking at each other, all thinking. These were all experienced journalists. Grounding the Delta fleet was an A1 story in any journalist's book. So what in God's name did Alec Haig think he was playing at . . .?

'I'm gonna get on the phone,' John Casserotto said. 'I'll bet a Delta's come down with a VIP on board. Burton and Taylor, they have a Delta, don't they?'

'Sit down, John, and use your loaf . . . Alec Haig wouldn't snow us like that. If a plane had crashed, he'd damn well tell us. And he'd tell us how and why. Whenever has that man ever tried to pull the wool over our eyes?'

'What are you, a public-relations man?' John sneered. But he didn't pick up the phone, and he did sit down. 'It just doesn't make sense,' he said.

It didn't of course. The tailplane modification story was true. Sir Barton had wanted the press to be told everything, had wanted names to be named. But Jacques and Alec had persuaded him to let them run the conference this way. They knew the agency men wouldn't believe the story, but it had the one virtue of being true.

The agency men talked the whole matter over. John Casserotto was all in favour of using the phone to blow the story, to do a speculative, 'What's gone wrong with Instecon?' But finally, the saner approach of Don Berrimore prevailed. He went to the door and called Alec Haig and Hank back into the room.

'You're a smart bastard,' Don said to Alec, 'and we've let off steam while you've been out of the room, but don't think we're going to buy your story. Because we're not. All right, so we believe you that while the planes are down on the ground you'll work on the tailplane assembly. You'll also empty the ash-trays and change the toilet paper in the loos. But what's the story beind the story, eh? We've drunk your booze in the past and eaten your cake, but we're working journalists, and I guarantee that if you don't come clean your company will be crucified . . .'

'That's a risk we have to take,' Alec said gravely. 'The Deltas are being grounded. I've given you a true reason why.'

'And so the sub-editor from the *Doncaster Bugle* or the *Poughkeepsie Echo* calls up one of your offices, talks to a mechanic, and get's the score. What kind of mugs does that make us look, eh? We've got to file a story in self-defence, you know that . . .'

'I can promise you that any story will come only from me, and I will give it only to you gentlemen,' Alec said.

'So there *is* a story?'

'I'm not saying that. I'm saying that nobody else in Instecon will say anything to the press.'

'Information can be bought . . .'

'Not from Instecon it can't,' Alec said. 'Not in this matter.'

'So there *is* a *story*?'

'No comment.'

'You said in your statement,' John Casserotto said, 'that Instecon was "co-operating with the airlines . . ." Does that mean that while the Delta is grounded, Instecon is going to pay to hire or lease substitute equipment? That would cost millions of dollars. Is Instecon paying all that money, Mr Haig, or not?'

'Trick question,' Alec said. 'No comment.'

'Would you deny that Instecon is going to force the share-holders of the airlines to bear the substantial cost of grounding the Delta? Would you agree that Instecon has a duty to help bear the cost?'

111

'No comment.'

'You realize I can't go back to my editor with a nine-liner and a free ballpoint pen?' John said stubbornly. He snapped his pad closed and made for the door. 'If you want my opinion,' he said, 'I think that statement stinks, and I for one don't buy it. Something's gone wrong with Instecon, and it's my job as a professional journalist to find out exactly what. Mr Haig, your shareholders have a right to the truth, and I intend to see they get it. It may surprise you to know that I am one of them . . .'

Don hastened across the room and took John's arm.

'Look, John,' he said, 'hang on a minute. Don't get mad and blow it. There's something behind all this. If we stick with it, we may get it.'

'Since when this all-pals-together act, Don? We're in competition, you and me, and don't forget it. Stick around here, if you want, but I believe the story's not in this office. Like, this isn't the scene, man . . .'

Alec saw him throw off Don's arm, and start to leave. 'If there's a story, John,' Alec called out, 'it'll be on the only Delta still to fly . . .'

John swivelled round. 'I thought you said they were all grounded?'

'Read your statement. Or are you so much of a journalist you don't bother with shorthand any more? What I said was all Deltas *in airline service* would be grounded. Instecon has its own Delta. If there is a story, I think it'll take place on the flight to Jamaica which our own Delta will be making tomorrow . . .'

'So I'll call New York and they'll have a stringer meet it . . .'

'Better still. If you run the statement I've given you today, I'll invite you on board that plane. Round trip to Montego Bay. And when the plane touches down at the end of the trip, I or my co-director M. de Blaie will answer any questions you may care to put to us . . .'

John Casserotto came back into the room. 'Making a deal, eh?'

'You could call it that.'

'Who else will be on the plane?' Don Berrimore asked. 'How many other journalists?'

'Just you five . . .'

They looked at each other. 'Suits me,' Arthur Verves said. Quickly the other two agreed. Don looked at John; between them they represented the two largest agencies in the most fiercely competitive business in the world.

Don stuck out his hand. 'It's a deal?' he asked.

They'd done it before on big stories, agreed to go along together.

'Okay,' John said, 'I could do with a trip to the sunshine . . .'

＊　　＊　　＊

Sally was waiting for Alec when he came to her apartment, high in the old house overlooking the lake. The house had no lift but he ran up the steps and arrived at her door without breathing heavily. He was a tall man, lithe, with no excess fat, moving gracefully as a leopard. She opened the door when he knocked on the bronze gargoyle knocker, and let him in. She was wearing a trouser suit; dark navy-blue trousers, a blue-and-white horizontally striped sweater, and a white coat over it, with large brass buttons, double breasted in a quasi-naval style.

'Ahoy there,' he said, and gave her a mock salute. That was

113

before he kissed her. She snuggled close to him. 'I suppose I should say, it's been a long time,' she said, 'but I won't. Every time you hold me and kiss me, I forget all the other times, and so it never seems like a long time . . .'

'And you a mountain spirit from Wales,' he said, 'with Dylan Thomas in your bloodstream, laver in your bones and a whole lifetime of bardic mysteries in the black pools of your eyes . . .' She shivered, held him close again. He could smell her perfume, feel her soft hair rubbing against his cheeks. She felt firm and strong and aggressively female, a woman who could give as much as she could take. He couldn't stand women who whined, who fluttered their eyelashes – usually false – ate honey and cream to pamper their powdered complexions. Sally had the healthy look of a girl who's just stepped off the ski slopes; she used hardly any face powder or lipstick, no eye make-up or rouge, and yet she always glowed with an inner love, exciting, interesting, full of comprehension. She could be tender too. She drew back from his arms. 'If you wanted to cancel our date,' she said, 'I'd understand. You must have an awful lot on your plate now we've grounded the Delta . . .'

He held her hand. 'That's all been taken care of,' he said. 'Dammit, what do we have a public relations department for? And an engineering department.'

'And a so-called technical sales department,' she said softly. The technical sales department covered a multitude of activities, as well they both knew.

She drew him slowly into the flat as they talked. The light from along the lake gleamed across the still sheet of water. In the window she'd placed a table, set for dinner, with candles which she had lighted. On a trolley beside the main table was a tray containing hors-d'œuvres; on another trolley was an old-fashioned cake, iced white, carrying one candle

114

only. Beside the cake was a bottle of Madeira wine and two glasses; a bottle of white wine was standing in an ice bucket beside the table. The apartment gleamed with soft light reflected from woodwork polished to a subtle hand-rubbed shine; the furniture was old, small unmatched pieces picked up in the shops around Zürich which blended in a tasteful scheme of decoration.

'I made a booking,' he said. 'At the Bauerschloss. I talked with the cook. Tonight they have a wonderful Kassler Rippchen . . .'

'I thought we might eat in,' she said.

'I didn't want to put you to all that trouble.'

'It's a pleasure to make a meal for you, where we can sit and look out over the lake, and watch the lights on the boat.'

The ferry boat sailed backwards and forwards across the tip of the lake, a ribbon of light that reflected off the rippling water, a silent movement that animated the entire landscape. They were too high to see or hear the cars which ran along the street; the ribbon of lights along the edge of the lake were hidden in the bare branches of the trees. The first snow had fallen on Uetliberg, and lights winked from chalets on the side of the mountain. He stood in the window while she moved silently before the hors-d'œuvre trolley, piling small portions from each of the dishes on to a plate. Then she put the plate on one side of the table, began quietly to fill a plate for herself. She was humming a Spanish melody, and spoke the words so clearly in her lilting Welsh voice that he could understand them. When she paused he took up the words, though he could not sing as she had done. 'You are like the Rose of Alexandria,' he said, 'white by day but coloured by night.'

Then both fell silent. The last stanza of the song, both

suddenly realized, said, 'Oh, of your love I am dying, since the first day we met . . .'

There was a knock on the door, and she went to open it. A beaming man was standing in the doorway; behind him two small boys carried a large metal box. She ushered the man inside and he shepherded the boys before him, carrying the box as if it contained the last egg of a dying breed of birds. Sally brought a stool and placed it near the table and the boys lowered the large metal box gently on to it, the man watching it down every centimetre of the way.

'Do you require anything further?' the man asked Sally, smiling conspiratorially. She thanked him in fluent French, which Alec noticed she now spoke without a trace of accent, and then she thanked the boys in *Schweizerdeutsch,* and the man and the boys left. One of the boys looked at Alec, and nearly winked . . .

Sally held out a chair, and Alec sat on it. The lake glittered to his left but when Sally sat opposite him he had no eyes for the water.

'What's in the box?' he asked casually, knowing the answer.

'Kassler Rippchen . . . from the Bauerschloss . . .'

He held out his hand and she gripped it. 'I bought you a present,' she said, 'and left it at the office! How's that for efficiency?' She laughed out loud. He squeezed her hand, seeing the brightness of her eyes near to tears.

'Being here with you is present enough . . .'

She laughed again, brittle as old thin glass. 'But I was going to give it to you and then say, 'since I've given you a present, will you give me a present?, and you would say "of course, what do you want?" and I'd say, "the best present you could give me would be to let me tell you how much I love you . . .!" There, I know we agreed we'd never talk like that together, that it was to be strictly for laughs, and we mustn't get

116

serious about each other, but there's no harm, Alec, in me telling you I love you . . .'

Now she was crying and his grip tightened on her hand, and she came out of her chair, and he half rose from his, and their heads met clumsily and they were kissing and she was crying on his face, and the warm sweet salt tears ran on to his lip. But somewhere deep inside himself he felt the start of that cold iron growth that always happened to him in the presence of love. Alec Haig had loved, once, and she had been killed, but the love he had felt had not died with her.

'Sally,' he said gently, and she heard the reproach in his voice even though he had tried to mask it. Her tears stopped falling. She ground her mouth into his. 'All right,' she said, 'if it can't be love, let it be something else. I want you. I want you.'

'I want you too,' he said, 'but I can't go on like this. You mean a hell of a lot too much to me to want to hurt you.'

She drew away from him. Not far away; just so that she could look at him. 'Nobody else, is there?' she asked, 'not that it's any business of mine.'

He shook his head.

'I know about the others,' she said. 'That airline hostess, what was her name . . .?'

'Micky . . .?'

'Yes, that's her. I'm jealous, of course, but like you, I believe nobody owns anybody.'

The supper momentarily forgotten, they sat on the sofa by the warm oil-burning stove.

'Let me explain something,' he said. 'This isn't something I've ever said before, and perhaps I won't be able to say exactly what is in my mind, but I'd like to try. I don't confuse love and sex,' he said. 'Sex is wonderful when two people care about each other, but it has nothing to do with love.

117

Love is wonderful between two people, but it doesn't depend on sex. I've only ever been in love once in my life. With the girl I married. She was by no means perfect. She had a lousy temper, she wasn't much of a cook, or a housekeeper, or good at making arrangements, or remembering dates, or times, or even names and places. But I loved her. And the crazy thing is, that even though she's been dead for so long that the memory of her face has faded from my memory, I think I still love her. It isn't very tactful of me to say that to you, but I felt I had to . . .'

'You're not a very tactful person, Alec. But you're always honest. But what would you say if I were to tell you I think I feel the same way about you. Ever since I met you first, back in Wales. Ever since that crazy trip to Tokyo, ever since you asked me to come to Zürich to work for you . . .'

'No man has any right to expect anyone to be as good as you are,' he said. It was perfectly true. She was a better secretary than any man could expect. They went to bed together sometimes, and that too was good, but now both of them knew that would have to be resolved, one way or the other.

'Do all your secretaries fall in love with you?' she asked softly.

'I've only ever had two,' he said.

'And the other left the company . . .?'

'Yes.'

'Did she love you?'

'I'm afraid so . . .'

'But she left the company. She knew the way you felt . . .?'

'I think so . . .'

She tucked her legs up on the sofa, between them. 'I'm not going to leave,' she said, 'but then I was brought up in a mining valley, and they breed us tough in Wales.'

'I can't change,' he said.

'Thank God for that. I'm not so sure I'd love you if you were different. Have your air hostesses, have anybody you like, except for one thing.'

'What's that?'

'Don't bring any of 'em to Zürich. I'll scratch their eyes out . . .'

*　　*　　*

About eleven o'clock that night, the industrial psychologist and the psychiatrist both agreed they'd had enough for one day and sent Willie Smedhurst off to his hotel to get some sleep.

They had filled in the details of Willie's day, up to the moment of him getting into that plane to start his check. What they knew about Willie Smedhurst would have filled a book; what they knew about the method of poisoning him wouldn't look out of place on a pin head. Willie went back to his hotel with his head in a whirl. Who could believe that Willie hated smoking, and only bought cigarettes at that one kiosk because he fancied the girl behind the counter? Who could have believed that the reason he hadn't asked the girl out was because of a lack of confidence in himself, caused by his knowledge that he spoke Italian with an English accent. And who could have believed that the reason he maintained his accent when he spoke Italian was because he used his 'foreignness' as a protection, since psychologically he was fighting absorption into a land other than the land of his birth. He, who had worked for Instecon all over the world, had wound that voice around himself, in Italian, Spanish, and German, as a chauvinistic protection against the society in which we live. The industrial psychologist had advised Willie strongly to apply for a job back in England; he felt that Willie's technical abilities eventually would become impaired by this chauvinism. The psychiatrist, however, had insisted that before he returned to England, he should take that girl from behind the cigarette kiosk and ask her, in whatever accent he chose to use, to go to bed with him. 'It won't matter if she accepts or refuses,' the psychiatrist had said, 'but at least you'll have given yourself the satisfaction of knowing that you were able to ask her. And then, perhaps, you'll stop buying cigarettes.'

By an unspoken agreement, neither man would discuss Willie Smedhurst after he had gone. The investigation was not yet complete and such theories as they had must remain as such. They left the Instecon building together and the staff car took them to the Central Hotel in which the company had booked a double bedroomed suite for their use. They ate supper together in the hotel dining-room which, at that hour, was quite deserted. They talked together about music, painting, and a performance of the Oberammergau play each had seen. After supper they retired upstairs to read, smoke, and relax before going to bed. At half past twelve the psychiatrist knocked out his pipe and declared himself ready for sleep.

'We shall have an interesting day tomorrow,' the industrial psychologist said. 'I think we shall have an opportunity of developing a little theory of mine.'

The psychiatrist, however, had already gone into his room. he reappeared almost instantly with a towel in his hands. 'Do you wish to use the bathroom first?' he asked, but the psychologist shook his head. 'I always bathe in the mornings,' he said, 'and I suppose we have an interesting comparison.

Some people prefer to go clean into the public world of the daytime, others to go clean to the private world of the bed...'

The psychiatrist laughed, but he went into the bathroom without replying, and shut the door. The industrial psychologist chuckled when he heard the lock snap shut; he'd had a little bet with himself that his distinguished colleague would do that. He went into his bedroom and without even washing or putting on pyjamas, he climbed into bed.

'Yes,' he said, continuing his previous thought before the psychiatrist locking the bathroom door had distracted him, 'I bet we'll have an interesting day tomorrow. I bet someone else has realized, as I have realized, that Willie Smedhurst is a compulsive pen-chewer. I wonder if we shall discover they substituted another pen for the one Willie had been using...?'

He put off his light, and fell instantly asleep.

PHASE 8

Theodore Charalambous Pappayanakis was known to his friends as Toni. A Cypriot Greek who owned a small garage in a village on the crest of a mountain overlooking Zürich, Toni was an electronic and mechanical genius who might have been worth a fortune if only his inventions could have been patented. They were inspired, however, and usually paid for, by Alec Haig. Toni had been the unit mechanic when Alec fought with the Long Range Desert Group, and had kept the unit wheels turning often with no more than the aid of a piece of wire, a screwdriver, and an inheritance of native cunning.

Toni's garage earned sufficient to satisfy his simple domestic tastes; he had no great love of the internal combustion engine, or the tin-box death-traps into which most modern manufacturers cram them and call them cars; he had nothing but contempt when the latest production model was wheeled in, often with water steaming out of its radiator, oil leaking from its crankcase, and petrol being emitted only partly burned from its exhaust. 'My God,' he'd say. 'Not another one of them. When are you idiots going to stop buying this rubbish . . .?' He became known throughout the district as a highly skilled mechanic, but 'a bit of a character'.

At Alec Haig's request, Toni invented a giro-mounted parabolic microphone. He took it with him when, again at Alec's request, he booked a winter holiday in Jamaica. He left the garage in the hands of the baker's son, a near idiot. 'No one will ever know the difference,' he said. 'Just tell 'em the first thing that comes into your head.'

A room had been booked for Toni at the Casa Negra in Montego Bay. When Willie met him at the airport, after he had cleared Customs with his parabolic microphone concealed inside a transistor radio, neither gave any sign of recognizing the other, though Willie had told the Chief Dispatcher he had been booked. Willie stowed Toni's two suitcases in the boot of the Lincoln and kept the transistor on the seat beside him. As the car pulled out of the airport, each identified himself to the other, using the Instecon code, and both relaxed.

But first Toni took a pencil from his top pocket, opened the top to reveal a micro-meter, and waved the pencil about inside the car. The micro-meter registered nothing. Willie watched him through the car mirror.

'May I ask what you looking for, sah?' he asked.

'To find if this car is safe.'

'Safe from what, sah?' Willie asked.

'From bugs.'

'Listening bugs, or biting bugs?'

'Either.'

Willie laughed. 'No bugs in Willie's car, sah,' he said.

'Good. How is your friend, the house-boy?'

'Dat one not my friend, sah. What for you call him my friend, sah? Dat one de bad man.'

'But he works for you?'

'No, him work for de money.'

'Can he swim?'

'Like a fish.'

'Can he sail a boat?'

'No, but I can teach him.'

'Can you teach me?'

'Willie can teach anybody. Tomorrow morning?'

'Today.'

'Willie can teach you.'

Toni booked into Casa Negra. The room had formerly been occupied by Alec Haig, but no sign of his attack remained. Toni changed out of his travelling clothes, put on a long-sleeved cotton shirt and a pair of tight shorts over his swimming trunks. On his feet, on Willie's advice, he wore skin-tight rubber slip-ons beneath his tennis shoes. 'You ever tread on a sea urchin you'll know why,' Willie said. While Toni was changing, Willie had been down to the town of Montego Bay, and had borrowed a boat shaped like a surfboard, on which a sail and mast were rigged. The mast and sail were collapsed and the boat sat neatly on his roof rack when he got back to the Casa Negra. They drove back in the direction of the airport, east along the coast road, a tourist going for a sail with a hired car and a hired sailboat. Half a mile past the Crescent Moon Hotel the house-boy was waiting, thumbing lifts from the passing cars, confident that none would stop except the one he wanted, the Lincoln driven by Willie. When the car halted he went to get in the back with Toni, but Willie opened the front door. 'In here with me, black trash,' he said. The house-boy climbed in and flashed a toothy smile at the white passenger in the back seat. Toni had been well briefed by Alec, knew this lad was in it for the money.

'What's your name, boy?' he said.

'Mr Christopher Dogley, sah,' the boy said.

'Then I'll call you Chris . . .'

'That's not my name, sah . . .'

'Would you rather I call you Dog?'

'You can call me Chris, sah.'

124

Willie took them along the coast past the Frobisher Place, past Rose Hall, and eventually stopped the car in a grove of palms, almost at the water's edge. Chris and Willie took the boat from the roof of the car and rigged it, and then Willie took them both out and taught them to sail. There was nothing to it, and within half an hour either one of them could handle the tiller, sail forward on either tack, turn the boat, and head it in any direction they chose. Then Willie taught Chris how to capsize.

At midday Chris set off on his own, sailing the boat westwards, tacking and veering in a most inexpert manner. When he arrived level with the Frobisher Place the boat seemed to go out of control, headed straight for one of the buoys from which the shark net was suspended, narrowly missed a collision, then jibed and ran straight in towards the shore.

Sam Bantam had been sitting on the terrace taking a pre-lunch drink when the sailboat drew level with the property. He had not paid it any attention, other than to remark to Veronica, sitting in the shade behind him, what a lousy sailor the guy was.

'Did you see that?' he exclaimed when the small craft jibed. 'If that guy isn't careful, he'll have that damn thing over.'

And then, as he predicted, the wind caught the boat, which began to heel further and further. The sailor leaned towards the mast instead of away from it. 'You crazy bastard,' Sam called derisively, 'lean back, you crazy bastard.'

But the boat continued to slip away, and then suddenly heeled completely over and the sailor took a dive head first into the water and they could just hear a thump, and the boat was down, the sail lying flat, and then sinking as the boat tipped completely upside down.

Sam and Veronica watched, Sam amused, Veronica uninterested. But after a minute, or so it seemed, Sam jumped to his feet.

'Goddamn it, Veronica, the guy hasn't come up,' he said.

Both saw the inert body of the sailor as it floated to the top of the water, lying still, face down.

Now Sam was shouting for Tobias, who came running from the back, and together they raced across the hot sand to the small boat moored near the water's edge. They jumped into it; the outboard motor mercifully fired first pull of the recoil starter and the boat roared towards the capsized sailboat. When they got there, the sailor was barely conscious, lying on his back, trying ineffectually to make a few swimming strokes. They dragged him into the runabout, and brought him back to shore, leaving the sailboat where it was. Tobias lifted him and carried him across the sand. 'Put him in the guest cabin,' Sam ordered. Tobias carried the sailor across the sand to the thatched-roof guest-house cabin beneath the stand of palms, and laid him out on the bed. Sam followed them in. Chris was moaning softly, but his eyes were partly open. 'Lie still for a while,' Sam said. 'You must have got a bang on your head when you went overboard. Don't worry, we'll get your boat in.'

Chris smiled his gratitude at them, closed his eyes. Tobias covered him with a sheet. 'Do you think we ought to get a doctor?' he asked, but Sam shook his head. They went out and closed the cabin door behind them. Sam sent Tobias out in the boat to fetch in the capsized sailboat, and went up to the veranda.

Veronica was looking paler than usual, though she had not moved from her seat in the shade. 'He'll be okay,' Sam said. 'Must have banged his head when he went overboard, that is all.'

126

'You're not going to let him stay here?' Veronica asked.

'He'll be okay in an hour or two. Poor bastard. Let him sleep it off, though why they let guys like that take out a sailboat beats me . . .' He came up on to the veranda and sat down again. Moisture was running down the side of his glass. 'Gimme some more of that ice, willya?' he asked. Veronica fished a couple of cubes from the ice bucket and dropped them into his glass.

'I've got a bunch of guys coming in on the afternoon plane,' he said, 'so I'm afraid I'll be tied up this evening.'

'Business or pleasure?'

'What's that to you, huh?'

'I just wondered.'

'So leave the wondering to me, huh? Just so long as you get yours regular, and I don't keep you short in that direction, eh, babe?'

She looked at him, slumped in his chair, his drink in hand, that terrible smirk on his face. If only he knew! He thought himself the ultimate in lovers because he gave her money when she wanted it, and lay on top of her, grunting and sweating like the pig he was, trying ineffectually to satisfy her cravings and bring her to orgasm. If only he knew that so far he hadn't aroused her once, and that every time she'd faked it. She could put on a great performance for him; she needed to; few men can face the truth about their lack of sexual prowess.

'What drives you along all the time, Sam?' she asked, genuinely curious. 'Anybody else would relax and take a proper vacation, but not you. You have people coming and going all the time. You talk to New York and London and Switzerland three or four times a day. I thought you were supposed to be taking a holiday?'

'You keeping track on me, or something?'

'No, Sam, I'm not keeping track on you. But I'm curious...'

'Curiosity killed the cat, babe . . .'

'But why, Sam, why?'

He reached over and took the bottle from the trolley. Bourbon. The very best kind in the square black bottle. He poured a generous helping in his glass without speaking and she dropped a couple of cubes of ice in with it. Bourbon on the rocks. In this heat! 'Look, Veronica,' he said when he had taken a drink, 'I'm not gonna give you the usual crap about big business. Some guys may be in it because of family, inherited wealth and all that shit. Some guys are in it because they were born on the Lower East Side, or in the Bronx, and they screwed and gouged and fought their way up, so now they've got the habit, and that's all they've got. But me, Veronica, I was born into a little money, not too little, not too much. My old man was a nice friendly guy who left me a small bundle, not like Rockefeller you understand, but enough to get by. But I like money, babe, like you like screwing, and making a buck gives me a feeling like nothing any woman ever did with her body for me . . .?'

'Don't I make you happy . . .'

'That's not what I'm saying, babe. Like you're great, one of the greatest.' He laughed coarsely. 'And worth every penny . . .' He laughed again. 'Making you is great, babe, but making a dollar is better . . . How about that Veronica, I made a funny, making you is great but making a buck is better . . .'

'You're full of laughs, Sam,' she said.

He finished his drink. 'Now I got to go, meet this coupla guys,' he said.

'How long will you be?'

'What's the matter. Getting hot for it again?'

'I miss you when you're gone . . .'

'Look, I'll only be gone a coupla hours. When I get back

we'll have lunch, and then, Sam'll look after you, babe, promise. Sam'll look after you but good.'

'I can hardly wait,' she said.

When Tobias returned from bringing in the sailboat, he put on his khaki trousers and denim shirt 'uniform' and brought the rented Cadillac from the garage with the air conditioning unit running. Sam had changed into a white shirt and a pair of dark blue trousers; he came through the veranda, squeezed Veronica's shoulder, got into the car and left. She rubbed her shoulder ruefully. 'Strong as a bull,' she thought, 'in all but the one vital part . . .'

The afternoon plane hadn't arrived yet. Who could he be going to meet? The New York plane arrived each afternoon at three o'clock, so he couldn't be going to meet it. She dismissed all thoughts of Sam. She waited ten minutes on the veranda, then went through into her bedroom and showered, washing her white skin with lemon-scented soap. She dressed without underwear in a cool thin kaftan robe Freddie Smythe had bought for her in Marrakesh and, wearing a wide-brimmed sun hat, walked slowly as a sleep-walker out of the house and across the strip of sand towards the guest house in which Tobias had put the sailor.

She stood outside the door under the shade of the thatched eaves, and listened. No sound came from within. She could hear the tonk-tonk of the bell bird from the patio outside the kitchen, but there was no other sound anywhere on the property. Cassie would be in the back of the main house, preparing lunch, carrying her two-years-old child everywhere she went. Tobias had driven Sam into the town. Cassie's sisters, who served at table, hadn't arrived yet and when they did they'd busy themselves laying the table on the mosquito-netted veranda on the other side of the house, out of the direct sunlight. The palm trees above the guest house

129

hut swayed in a light breeze, and Veronica shuddered with all her being.

She opened the door and went in.

He was lying on the bed, flat on his back, as she had seen him several times before. His eyes were closed, but that was an old trick. She wanted to turn and run out of the guest house; she felt the familiar feeling of disgust rising in her, but some force stronger than her will propelled her towards the bed.

His eyes flicked open, and he smiled at her.

'I was right,' she said, 'it *was* you.'

'Yes, it's me.'

'I recognized you . . .'

'I hoped you might.'

'It wasn't an accident.'

'What do you think?'

'If you wanted to come here, you didn't need to capsize a boat. You could have come through the gate . . .'

'I doan't think the Massa would have had me placed into a bed in the guest house, if I'd come through the gate . . .'

'Too damn right he wouldn't. He'd have thrown you out.'

'That is what I supposed!'

Now she was near the bed, but he didn't move.

'What are you doing here?' she asked. Oh God, why had he come? Everything had been all right with Sam. Certainly, he was a grunting pig of a man and nauseated her in bed, but she was building a cache of money and soon would have enough to tell him to start screwing himself and she could go back to Europe. She longed for Europe, for London, the South of France, Rome, her familiar hunting grounds.

'What were you doing on a boat anyway?'

She looked down on him on the bed, covered with a single sheet; he grinned insolently up at her, and she shivered seeing the pink inside of his mouth and his pink tongue.

'I went sailing . . .'

'Why past here?'

'You know.'

'That's all finished.'

Now she was touching the side of the bed, leaning her weight against it. The sheet was pulled tight around his body and she could see the shape of him.

'Is it?'

She was breathing deeply, looking down at the muscles along his shoulder uncovered by the sheet, remembering the smoothness of his skin, smelling the sweet warm feral odour emanating from him.

'You know it's finished. I gave you all my money.'

He looked up at her face, his eyes caressing her lips, watching her sharp white teeth bite nervously at the tip of her tongue, feeling her eyes on his mouth.

'It isn't money with me any more,' he said.

'You had plenty off me . . .'

'Yes, but that was only at the start. We missed you.'

'We?'

'Me and him.' He beckoned with his hand in a gesture that could have been coarse but wasn't.

She shuddered, remembering.

'That white man you living here with,' he said, his eyes glinting. 'Is it good with him? Good as it was with me?'

'I don't have to pay him.'

'You don't have to pay me. Not now.'

She laughed, nervous, brittle. Her eyes were hungry, her mouth was hungry, her body leaned hungrily forward against the bed.

'Then you must have changed,' she said. 'It was always money first, with you. Money first. You were mad for money, a devil for money.'

He looked up at her, smiled a slow smile, stretched his arms free of the sheet. 'Like I said, White Lady, we missed you, him and me.'

When he had finished with her she was moaning in ecstasy, and wearing a gold locket Theodore Charalambous Pappayanakis had brought from Switzerland.

The locket had been Alec Haig's idea; the ecstasy was a touch which Chris added, all by himself. After all, why share the money he'd been given with a bitch, a white one at that, when you can pay her off by other methods?

PHASE 9

Night falls suddenly in the tropics, and the light of day fades rapidly to the silky dark of the evening. A million flowers wait for the last rays of light to disappear, and then spray the perfumes they have created all day inside themselves; the air is laden with the odours of gardenia and frangipani, oleander, orange blossom, musk and verbena.

Toni rose slowly out of the water. He'd paddled along the coast line wearing a breathing mask and flippers like fins. Most of the time he'd swum gently, using a long, slow side stroke learned in the waters of his native Cyprus. He took off the flippers and the mask, laid them by the water's edge near the artificial diving platform of the swimming pool. He walked slowly across to the house. Sam Bantam and his guests were eating dinner in the screened veranda on the other side of the house, and no one was interested in this part. He walked up to the veranda from which Sam had watched Chris capsize the sailing boat. The ice bucket was still on its pedestal.

He took the magnetic microphone from the waterproof pocket of his swimming trunks, unwrapped it from its polythene bag, and stuck it beneath the bucket. He snapped his fingers near to it, then snapped them about three feet away from it. Each time he snapped his fingers, a light winked on a boat out beyond the shark net buoys. He went back to the door of the veranda and clicked it. The light winked again.

He walked back down the beach, taking care to keep out of the sight line of the screened veranda on the other side of the house, put on his mask and flippers, and slipped back into the sea. He swam along the coastline for about ten minutes, round the promontory. The water was cooler than it had been during the day, but still warmer than was comfortable for swimming. He had the sensation of perspiring into the salty ocean water, turned over on his back, and rested while he floated. The salt water was more buoyant than he had been accustomed to, and floating on it was somehow awkward, but he paddled slowly along until the dark shape of the boat came within his view. Willie was on board, rowing firmly by stirring the water off the stern with one paddle.

Toni climbed into the boat, slumped down on the seat.

Willie handed him the thermos flask of coffee and Toni drank some of it from the cup which fitted its neck. 'Rum be better,' Willie said, but Toni shook his head.

He leaned forward and turned the switch on a black box on the other seat of the boat. Beside the box was a tape recorder, and he had watched the wheels whirring. They could hear a voice, two or three voices close to the microphone. 'She's wearing the locket,' he said. Willie nodded. 'I been recording every word dey speak,' he said.

Toni left the seat and erected a fishing pole at the back of the boat. 'You can start the engine now.'

Willie pulled the cord of the outboard motor. It took three pulls. Toni sneered at it. 'Valve needs grinding,' he said almost automatically. They trawled the boat along the water with the fishing rods hanging over the back. Several other boats were on the water, some of which had a white man fishing and a black man steering. The boat coasted slowly beneath the Jamaican night sky until it was level with the Frobisher Place, just off the line of buoys that marked the shark net, just another boat out in the night, fishing for whatever it could catch. Around them Toni could see the other boats, many carrying a small light, all of them with fishing lines streaming out into the water behind them. Willie manœuvred the boat until they were almost touching the buoy opposite the centre of the curved beach of the Frobisher Place then reached out, grabbed the buoy and drew them near to it. No one would be able to see from the shore exactly what they were doing. The buoy stood eighteen inches out of the water, and had no light on it. It gave a hollow clunk when Toni tapped it with his hand. 'Damn lucky it's not made of polystyrene or fibreglass,' he said, but Willie understood nothing of such technical matters. 'Magnets only stick to iron,' Toni explained. From the canvas bag at his feet he took out the parabolic microphone which he clipped to a three-legged stand. The bottom of each leg was magnetized, and the stand clamped to the buoy with a firm click. He tested it with his hand, and the stand didn't slip. He crouched down in the gunwales of the boat and peered through the aperture and the sights fixed to the microphone itself, unscrewed two knurled wheels and swung the microphone like a gun, pointing it at the Frobisher Place, towards the centre of the beach. Once it was set, he screwed the knurled wheels, tightening the microphone on that arc. He let go of the buoy and watched the microphone. No matter which way the buoy bobbed, no matter how quickly, the microphone continued to point at the same place, the centre of the beach, never varying by as much as a degree. Then he unscrewed another knurled wheel and looked through the aperture and the sight, pulling the sight back until he could see the entire beach from left to right, from water-line to the house.

That microphone had been developed to record bird

song; it could hear the cheep of the first cuckoo in spring from half a mile if it was correctly pointed. Now he had widened its angle, it would pick up any voice on that beach with clarity. The microphone was attached to its own battery-operated transmitter; in the boat he had a receiver which could take the input of three microphones, the one nestling between Veronica's breasts, the one under the ice bucket, and the parabolic on the buoy. Willie let in the clutch, and the boat chugged away from the buoy about five hundred yards. Then he switched off the motor, and they sat on the seat of the boat astern, listening to the dinner which Sam was giving for his friends. The output of the receiver was simultaneously being fed to a battery-operated tape recorder; every banal word was being recorded for posterity, and Alec Haig.

During dinner nothing extraordinary was said. It became apparent that Sam and Veronica had three male guests and three female guests, and their conversational level was that of high-school boys on week-end away from home. Mostly they told feeble and smutty stories to each other, and much laughter was generated, most of it forced.

At the end of dinner, the men left the covered veranda and the girls, and Toni switched to the ice bucket microphone.

No dirty stories were told. Sam poured each man a drink, and they sat in a circle round the centre table, with the ice bucket and the microphone ideally placed to hear every word that was said.

In the pause while the men came from one room to the other, Toni had changed the cassette in the recorder.

The men seemed to have one spokesman, who was asking for a further sum of money 'on account'.

Sam didn't want to cough up any more money.

136

'How do I know the damn thing works?' he said.

The spokesman patiently explained to him. 'It wasn't our fault some man chose that flight from Rome on which to have a burst appendix. By rights that plane should have been at thirty thousand feet. Even so, the plane went to the end of the runway, and if it hadn't been delayed by the tower, it would have been half-way through take-off when the electrics failed.'

How could Sam be certain the electrics had failed because of what they told him, and not because of some ordinary mechanical trouble? They had a deal and a deal was a deal. Two thousand sterling each in advance and they'd already had that. Five thousand sterling each when a Delta fell out of the sky. Well, it hadn't fallen out of the sky, had it? And the balance when it was proved that the plane had not been tampered with, when it became 'apparent' the plane had failed because of a design fault.

'Look here, you guys,' Sam said. 'If all I wanted to do was bring a plane down, I could have planted a guy on board with a bomb. Or I could have put a bomb in somebody's baggage. That's too easy. So far as I'm concerned, you guys can't have any more money until a Delta comes out of the sky from natural seeming causes. And that means no bombs, no hijacks, nothing the investigators can find . . .'

They argued some more, and finally Sam gave in. 'Okay, a thousand each, sterling, and two thousand to Samy here, for the expenses fund.'

Toni made a note of the name, Samy, which for once Sam Bantam had pronounced s.a.y.m.y. If he'd heard the name before, he must have confused it with a diminutive of Sam's own name. Once he had identified that name, he quickly identified the others. Ben and Arthur. For a time he had thought another man was present when Sam Bantam used the name Art, but quickly he realized that Sam was making his own diminutive.

After a while, Sam Bantam said it was time he took a walk, 'to spring a leak'.

Samy said he'd go with him.

Arthur said he'd go too.

Sam told Arthur where the bathroom was, then he and Samy went off the microphone in the ice bucket.

Toni switched to the parabolic, and picked them up, loud and clear, walking down the veranda steps. Looking towards the house from the boat he could see them silhouetted against the house lights as they walked towards the water. They were not speaking, but the microphone was so sensitive it picked up the crunch of their feet on the sand, like an army marching through dry snow. It picked up all the sounds of their activity once they reached the water's edge.

'That guy Art,' Sam said. 'I have him figured for a trouble-maker. You sure you can handle him?'

'Yes, I can take care of him.'

'Well, do that.'

'I'd have done it long ago, but we may need him. He's the one who fixed the plane in Rome while it was in the hangar.'

'The other guy, Ben, he's a nonentity. You gonna keep him? Or do you need him too?'

'Yes, *I* need *him*,' Samy said. Even on the microphone one could hear an edge to his voice.

'Whaddya mean, *I* need him?' Sam asked, suddenly suspicious.

'He's my insurance. It occurs to me that when we do this job you're going to have to pay us a lot of money. And we're going to know a lot about how you work. That knowledge might prove embarrassing to you, and you might want to do something about it. And save yourself some money.'

138

'Now see here. Whatever you may think of my business methods, I'm a straight-shooting guy. Sure I know you could embarrass me if any of this ever got out. That's what I'm paying you such a helluva lot of money for. If you do the job right. But a word of warning; get rid of them two guys, and don't try to cross me in any way, okay?'

'Okay.'

'Right. So how do you plan to do the job?'

'That's my business.'

'But it's gonna look natural, for Christ's sake?'

'Trust me . . .'

'I have to, haven't I? There's only one goddamned Delta in the air at the moment, so it has to be that one.'

'That's right. And we're all laid on to do the job right here, in Jamaica. We'll let the plane get here. That'll make 'em confident. And then we'll bug the plane, right here. It'll never get back to London.'

They stood side by side, and the noise of their activity sounded like a cataract on the parabolic microphone.

'Heavy drinkers,' Willie said, but Toni shushed him. They were speaking again.

'It doesn't bother you,' Sam was asking, 'knocking a plane-load of people out of the sky?'

'Bother me? Why should it. Just so long as I get my money . . .'

'After Algeria, you have a lot of hate in you, Samy.'

'Does that bother you?'

'Not at all. That's why I chose you. It cost me a bundle to look at the Instecon files in Zürich, and find you three guys. Instecon does a good job; that psychiatrist's report on each employee is invaluable. And so quick . . . I punched three facts on to the computer: technical ability, a history of financial problems (i.e. people who at some time or other

139

had needed to ask the company for a loan), and a suggestion of emotional instability. The computer dropped out your names in two minutes flat. And did you know, it also recommended you shouldn't be employed in a sensitive job?'

'Don't forget that third one, Sam, the emotional instability. That's the computer's way of warning you, don't screw around with us. We're nuts, and likely to go off bang, right in your face.'

The microphone picked up the sound of Arthur's voice as he walked down the beach towards them; it also picked up the tone of his suspicion and truculence. 'Right bloody millionaire's paradise you've got here,' he said.

'Sure is, Art. Feel like a swim?'

'Nor for me, thank you. The only swimming I do is in my bath on a Friday night.'

Sam guffawed to hide his embarrassment. 'Go on in, Art, the water's warm.'

'Not for me, thank you. Too many bloody sharks out there in the water. Not to mention a few back here on dry land.'

Sam laughed again, clapped his arm round Arthur's shoulder, and Samy's. 'Okay, boys,' he said, 'let's wrap it up, shall we? Spend the rest of the evening enjoying ourselves. The broads come with the compliments of the house, and believe me they're great, just great.'

'Tried 'em all, have you?' Arthur sneered.

'You might say that, Art. You might just say they all come with my personal guarantee.'

✳   ✳   ✳

When they went inside, Toni switched back to the ice-bucket microphone; it was picking up well though not so crisply as the parabolic. The girls came to join the men.

'Let's all go to the Yellowbird,' Veronica suggested, but Sam shouted his disapproval. 'The Yellowbird, babe, what the hell . . . what can we do there we can't do here in greater comfort except watch a lot of black assed bastards prance around. Okay, everybody, get your clothes off . . .'

Toni switched off the microphone.

Which was a pity. He missed what Sam later drunkenly called, the best, the biggest goddam gang bang he'd had since he was in college and they raided the gamma gamma gamma sorority house. He also missed a suggestion which Arthur, whose heart wasn't in sex games, made to Samy. At that moment Samy was heavily involved and breathing deeply. 'Yes, yes,' he said to Arthur, 'but now, do me a kindness and go away.'

Nobody ever knew what happened to Chris. He rented a boat shortly after dark. He'd been at the Yellowbird all evening and had drunk three-quarters of a bottle of Appleton rum. He'd paid for it in cash; and was wearing a smart suit.

'I'll show the bitch,' he said, as he lurched out of the club.

He'd gone down to the water's edge and had borrowed a sailboat. There'd been an unusual wind that late evening and early night, what the locals call a twister, since it blows this way and that, twisting in and out of the island coves.

They found the sailboat upturned, outside the shark net.

They never found Chris.

'A fish out dere has a pain in de belly,' Willie remarked when he heard the news.

*   *   *

When the Instecon Executive Delta took off the following afternoon, on the flight to Montego Bay, it contained sixty invited passengers. They were drawn from the boardrooms of historic merchant houses, leading commercial banks, Wall Street and the Stock Exchange, Lloyds of London; there were three German barons, the scion of one of the oldest families in Boston, two Italian princes, three French *comtes* and a *duc,* an English duke, four lords and three baronets. There was a Broadway producer, an American orchestral conductor, a former Hollywood film mogul now resident in Spain, and a South African diamond miner. The owner of one of the world's largest breweries in Milwaukee was there with his counterpart from Denmark, and a Finnish publisher who owned extensive timber interests.

A snack was served on the crested de Blaie family gold plate. Sir Barton supplied the glassware reputed to have been cut for an English queen by a Polish royal suitor. (She had accepted the glass but rejected his hand.) The snack was a simple pâte, a water ice, casserole of pheasant, and a choice of cheeses. Alec chose the wines from the Instecon boardroom cellar, including a venerable brandy. Sir Barton refused to permit port to be served on the plane, even though it was to be decanted before being taken on board. 'There are some things', he said, 'you just do not do. And taking an old port to thirty thousand feet is one of them.'

London Airport had been a battlefield when the Instecon

Delta took off; but the secret of its destination was safely guarded. Alec Haig and George Mason checked the plane together before take-off, and Professor Baxter himself observed them while they were doing it, interrupting the check frequently to take pulse, heart, and skin-temperature readings. The plane itself had been examined completely, from tip to tail, and a squad of Instecon guards then stayed with it every moment until it prepared for take-off.

Professor Baxter rode in the cabin with the pilot and the co-pilot, who was also fully qualified. During the flight Alec Haig and another qualified pilot would sit near the front of the plane ready to take over should they be required. All four had been tested before take-off; the possibility of a slow acting poison had not been overlooked but nothing was discovered.

Nevertheless, as the plane began to scream down the runway Alec found himself sweating slightly. 'It's all in the mind,' he told himself grimly, and forced himself to relax. Gradually, once the plane had snatched itself into the air, his brow dried again. He unfastened his seat belt, glanced round at the passengers. Was he right in taking risks with so many people? He would have preferred to fly the airplane alone, rather than run risks with other people's lives, but a solo flight to Jamaica would do little for the reputation of the company. Sixty 'I was there' stories were needed from impeccable sources, sixty testimonials that the plane flew well. But it was a helluva responsibility to bear, Alec was thinking. He walked through to the pilot's cabin, donned a pair of headphones and plugged himself into the intercom. Professor Baxter seized his wrist and felt his pulse. The skipper turned round and made the thumbs-up sign. Alec's eyes ran along the control dials and switches. Though he knew everything was in order, still he needed to reassure

143

himself. Once again he pressed the switch that revealed the pressure maintained by the bi-metal. Fifty pounds per square inch. Dead on the nose. He reached across the co-pilot and without warning switched off the starboard outer engine. The co-pilot and the skipper both shot a hurried look at him, astounded.

Warning lights flicked along the control panel. Even as the skipper had looked at Alec, automatically his hand had gone to the button marked 'emergency trim'. The computer came into operation, and apart from a slight downward dip, it corrected the functioning of the plane, held it to a steady course.

Meanwhile the computer brain was feeding along the line, seeking out the source of the engine fault, checking the thousand and one things that could be wrong. As the computer tested each section, and found it working correctly, a green light came on above each red warning light, showing there was no fault in that section of the mechanism. Finally, only one red had no green above it. The switch marked ON/OFF. The skipper pointed to that particular light and turned to Alec. The whole process had taken five and a half seconds, but during that time the plane had travelled over a mile and a half.

'It took its time,' Alec grumbled.

'Be fair. That switch is last in line. It had to go through the entire routine . . .'

'We must change the programme,' Alec said, 'that switch ought to be first in line for testing, not last . . .'

He pressed the switch into the ON position, and the computer put out all the green and red lights as it set about the complicated process of starting the engine again. The engine fired within two and a half seconds.

At least, Alec thought, we could maintain flight even with

an engine missing. Professor Baxter tapped him on the arm and they switched their headsets to 'interconnect' so they could talk privately together. 'Why don't you come back with me, sit down and relax?' the Professor said. 'Nothing's wrong with the plane . . .'

Alec had kept his promise and the only reporters on board were those who had attended the press conference in Zürich. They had played ball with him, and though the press of the world carried the story of the grounding of the Delta on its front page, a 'what's happened to Instecon' leader, and feature articles which compared the situation to that which had faced Rolls-Royce, no 'official' comment had been made since no one of substance could be found to act as spokesman for the company. The rumour-mongers and gossip columnists had a field day.

Alec tried hard to relax during the flight, but when the steward came back to inform him they were going into the landing pattern, he felt no relief, only a renewed sense of danger. A plane has two 'moments of risk' – take-off and landing. They'd got up into the air all right. But could they get down? He forced himself to stay in his seat. The plane was in better hands than his. He felt rather than heard the landing wheels go down, felt the plane slip slowly and inexorably towards the ground. 'Relax,' he told himself, 'the computer can't make a mistake.' Perhaps the pilot was landing the plane himself. Well, why not? He was an experienced flier, better than Haig himself. 'There's nothing you can do, Alec,' he told himself over and over again. The professor was looking at him, observing him closely. He managed a smile, but his face, despite being covered in sweat, felt as if it could crack. And then, through the windows, he saw the terminal buildings rushing past, felt the feather light touch of wheels on the tarmac, and blew out his breath in an audible gasp.

The plane and its contents had been insured at a premium of £400,000. The agent for the insurance company was waiting at the airport with an international satellite telephone line open to his head office. When the plane touched down he screamed into the telephone, 'It's down, it's down, safe and sound!' The chairman of the Insurance Company was heard to murmur, 'And a jolly good thing too!' Several members of Lloyd's permitted themselves a smile when they heard the news of the safe landing, but glanced uneasily at the Lutine Bell.

Every available Rolls, Bentley, Cadillac, Lincoln and Mercedes on the island had been pressed into service, and the airport porters issued with new white uniforms. The chief Customs officer glanced uneasily at the distinguished customers, then selected the English duke and asked him to open his bag. The duke was travelling with the most alarming pair of pop-art pyjamas, but did not seem the least embarrassed when they were exposed. After that the chief Customs officer waved them all through, smiling and saying 'Welcome to Jamaica, my lord,' to each one, regardless of rank.

Even Alec was given the same greeting, though the chief Customs officer had seen him many times.

Thirty girls had been flown from Instecon Offices all over the Caribbean, North and South America, including the redoubtable Madonna, who acted as chief organizer, chaperone, and den mother. The girls had collected in Miami, where Madonna had equipped them with identical outfits of matching pale blue smock and mini-skirt, a long white gown for evening wear, dark blue shorts and a white sleeveless shirt for day wear, and a black two-piece swimsuit. The girls were waiting at the Casa Negra, which had been taken over completely for the trip.

146

Only Alec Haig and Jacques de Blaie were there from the Instecon board; Kenneth Severs and Sir Barton Underwood stayed within reach of the markets, ready to instruct their brokers if the jobbers should bring the price down even lower than the 180.65 that had been quoted when the market opened. Even at that low price, there had been no takers, and the jobbers had been caught in a bull market. Only the options the Instecon board members individually had taken were holding the market steady, but it was a crisis situation of unprecedented proportions.

On the transatlantic flight, apart from serving a meal and such drinks as were requested, the Instecon personnel had deliberately left the passengers alone. Newspapers were supplied, and the weekly news magazines, but there was no folder of Instecon information, no glossy portraits of the plane and its unique history. Alec Haig held his first 'conference' early in the evening of the plane's arrival in Montego Bay. All the passengers had rested; some had swum, some sailed, others taken trips in the motor boats and glass-bottomed craft through which the coral reefs could be viewed. The car fleet had been at their disposal and some had taken a ride into Montego Bay, others around the hills to look at the superb Jamaican scenery and vegetation. It was a very relaxed meeting, held at one end of the dining-room of the Casa Negra, on the open-air patio where in the evenings a native band played and the limbo dancers performed. A table had been placed on the bandstand, and Alec sat behind it with Hank Dawson. The Instecon girls passed among the guests, handing out drinks. Alec had a small microphone on the table in front of him; his speech began: 'Your Highnesses, your Graces, my lords, ladies, and gentlemen . . .'

There was instant silence.

'First of all, our company would like to say how grateful

we are that each of you could spare the time to make this trip with us on the Delta aircraft. Our purpose in inviting you is quite simple and straightforward. We wanted you to experience a flight on board the Delta aircraft; we know that the conditions aboard that plane were somewhat, er, shall I say, more contrived than those an airline using the plane in day-to-day service is able to provide, but the basic plane is the same whether you fly it as our guest or as a regular passenger on a scheduled flight. And now, your itinerary whilst you are our guests. This again is quite simple. There is no itinerary. The Delta plane will take off for London at nine o'clock on the morning of the day after tomorrow. This will give you this evening and the whole of tomorrow in which to do exactly as you please. We have arranged a number of escorts for you, and golfing, fishing, cruising, swimming, surf-boarding, or just lazing on the beach or on your terraces, eating and drinking, are all available. Gentlemen, enjoy yourselves, relax, and don't spend too long in the sun without a hat . . .'

He switched off the microphone.

Oddly enough, it was Beresford Tomlinson, the agency man who'd had least to say in Zürich, who sprang to his feet. 'Mr Haig, on behalf of the press, may I ask when you're going to give us a proper press conference?'

Alec smiled at him. He hadn't dared hope he'd get away with it as easily as that, but the issue had to be faced, and he might just as well face it now and get it over with. He switched on the microphone. 'We can have a press conference anytime you boys want, Beresford,' he said. Then he addressed the other guests. 'What follows now, gentlemen, may be a little technical, and any of you who don't wish to stay obviously need not do so.'

A dozen or so of the guests got up and left. The rest took another drink, sat back, relaxed, and prepared to enjoy themselves. The five press men found seats near the front and were immediately given notepads and pencils by a girl to whom Hank nodded.

'One thing we've got to say, Hank,' Tim Bolton said with a friendly laugh, 'you sure know how to organize things . . .' Hank smiled, but didn't speak.

'Now, chaps, who goes first?' Alec asked.

Arthur Verries raised his hand. They'd done a deal, questions strictly in rotation. 'Why has the Delta fleet been grounded?'

Alec smiled. He'd expected that one to come first. 'I have nothing to add to the statement made to you in Zürich, but if you wish I'll read the statement again.'

'That won't be necessary.'

Don Berrimore second. 'It is being said that the Delta plane doesn't fly very well. Have you any comments to make?'

'You've just flown in one. I leave you to judge for yourselves.'

John Casserotto next. 'It's being said that there's a basic fault in the design of the Delta. If I might quote a leading Italian newspaper, whose name I can't remember since they don't take our service . . . The Delta is a flying death-trap . . . What do you say to that one . . .?'

'You've flown in the Delta, John, and you're not dead.'

Tim Bolton. 'Your share price has gone way down. Any comments to make on why?'

Now all the guests were interested. Each of them was materially and financially involved in the answer to this question. Alec looked around the room. This was the one to answer, without prevarication, without dodging the issue. 'Yes, Tim, I *can* tell you why,' he said slowly, 'but this is the way I'd like to do it. I'd like to tell you exactly why the share price is down. And then, I'd like to be excused from

149

answering any more questions until we arrive in London, the day after tomorrow.'

'But you'll make a complete statement now?' John Casserotto asked.

'Yes, as complete as I know how . . . Is that okay by everybody?'

The press men looked at each other. They had not spent the afternoon acting like tourists; they'd been locked together on Don Berrimore's balcony. 'Listen, fellows,' he'd said, 'I believe we're on to a big story here, a real world-beater. So don't let's foul it up by asking a lot of damned stupid silly questions. Just for once in a while, let's bury the hatchet, and all work together on this one.' John Casserotto had blown his stack, but eventually had been made to agree by force of numbers.

The press men nodded. 'But make it good, willya,' John Casserotto said plaintively, 'we're holding five open lines to New York at this moment.'

Alec paused a moment. It wasn't a conscious act of drama, but it brought the tension on that patio to electric pitch. The girls who had been moving among the guests with drinks stood stock still; the waiters behind the bar in the corner stopped shaking the mixers and switched off the machines in which they'd been preparing rum punches. Except for the bell bird in the tree, the patio was silent; then even the bell bird flew away.

'Somebody, and please don't ask me who, is spreading a false story that the Delta is a faulty plane, and that Instecon is cheating on its maintenance. Unfortunately this story has been believed in certain quarters, and sales of Instecon International shares have depressed the market value. There is no truth in this false story, none whatsoever. There is nothing wrong with the Delta, and nothing wrong with

150

Instecon's maintenance. We know there is an international scare about the stability of our company, and our ability to manufacture airplanes which fly. We hope that when you all get back to London, you will be able to verify that the Delta is an airworthy craft. We further anticipate that the market value of our company, and the value of its shares, will soon rise to a more equitable level. And that, chaps, is absolutely all I'm prepared to say at this moment.'

'Can we attribute that statement to you, Mr Haig, as a spokesman, or as a director of the company?'

'You can quote me if you like . . .'

'I accuse . . .?'

'There is a precedent even for that headline,' Alec said, smiling. But when he switched off the microphone, all present knew he would not switch it on again.

* * *

When news of the dramatic accusation was printed, the editors of the world's press said 'Nuts', and the share price fell a further ten points.

* * *

Willie's cousin was on duty on the pier by the Yacht Club, where the *Liberty Belle* was moored. Willie was driving the Lincoln and stopped it near his cousin.

'You wanta do a job for me, man?' Willie asked his cousin, when he stepped up to the car.

'Sure, Willie, what kinda job?'

'Take my car and go to Ocho Rios, pick up a message, an' bring it back here?'

'Aw, shit,' his cousin said, 'I be all day duty here.'

'What kinda duty you call dis? Somebody gonna come and take away de boat? Look, I'll stay here and look after de boat for you.'

'What for you doant wanta go to de Ocho Rios yourself, man?'

'You want de job or doan't? Take de car, and de job pay ten pounds Jamaican.'

'Aw, shit. Look after de boat.'

Willie's cousin took the car, and drove rapidly away. Willie watched him go, disapproving as the tyres bit into the dust. Five minutes later, Alec Haig and Antonio Giovanni walked on to the pier, straight past Willie, and on to Sam Bantam's boat. It was a luxurious cruiser, with six bunks in the main cabin and a double bunk in the forward cabin. The boat was fitted with every modern aid, radio, ship-to-shore telephone, radar, and asdic. In the after hatch, reached by a short stairway from the main cabin, was an engine-room containing four diesel engines, two banks of two.

'My God,' Giovanni said. 'It's like a navy destroyer.'

Giovanni worked for Instecon all over the world, nominally in the technical sales department. He and Toni had a close relationship, since he was usually the one to use the devices Toni made. To avoid confusion, Antonio was always given his full name. He was carrying a number of devices in his pocket, all of which had been constructed by Toni in his garage in Switzerland. Round his waist Antonio wore a belt which contained sets of spanners, metric, whitworth, and AF. He took off his belt, selected a whitworth spanner and un-

152

screwed the feed to each fuel injector. Then he took off the nuts that held the injectors into the cylinder block and removed the injectors themselves. They were all beautifully clean. 'He looks after his engine well,' Antonio said; 'give him credit for that.'

'I get the feeling that everything Mr Bantam does he does thoroughly,' Alec said. From his pocket, Antonio took a number of flat, thin wafers Toni had supplied. They were perforated in the centre, and explosive. He took a pair of scissors from his belt.

'Here we go again,' he said. 'Let's hope once again that our dear friend Toni knows what he's doing.' He took the scissors and held them against the capsule, ready to cut.

'If you want to go ashore, I don't mind,' he said, knowing full well that Alec would stay with him. He pressed on the scissors and, when nothing happened, he slowly cut the wafer into a circle slightly smaller than the end of the fuel injector. While he was fixing that one in place he handed the scissors and the wafers to Alec, who trimmed the rest of them to size. Antonio put a wafer on the end of each injector before he screwed it back into the cylinder head, then he reconnected the fuel feed lines, and pumped the primers to make certain the fuel would still flow and remove any air locks. To rig each engine took less than ten minutes; they were clear of the boat before Willie's cousin arrived in Ocho Rios to claim the sealed packet with the 'Come to Jamaica' poster in it which Willie had ordered by telephone.

Next time the engines of *Liberty Belle* were started, they would run quite normally until the ends of those nozzles reached a certain temperature. That would take approximately twenty minutes, by which time the boat would be clear of the port. When the capsules became hot enough they would

153

explode, and blow the engines out of the bottom of the boat.

*   *   *

Samy persuaded Arthur Lovell to go out in the motor boat. 'Poor bugger, I should think you're worn out,' Arthur said, glancing at Samy's chosen girl. The boat zoomed past the buoy carrying the parabolic microphone, but neither glanced at it. When they were half a mile out to sea Samy stopped the engine. Arthur wasn't surprised; he'd guessed this was no pleasure trip.

'When this is over,' Samy said, 'they're going to be looking for us if that device of yours doesn't work.'

'It'll work. Guaranteed. That plane'll drop out of the sky like a ruptured seagull, right over the middle of a lot of bloody deep water.'

'But if it doesn't work, they'll be looking for us. That Alec Haig, he's no mug, you know.'

'I know. That's why I'm bloody glad he'll be on the plane.'

'If they were to catch Ben here on the island, they'd think it was him, wouldn't they? They wouldn't look for anybody else. We would carry on with our jobs. If it didn't work, we wouldn't have any more money from Sam Bantam, and we'd need our jobs. Ben could be a sort of insurance for us, if you're game. It's worth thinking about, isn't it?'

He started the engine and they went back to shore.

*   *   *

For Toni's use and as protection against the fierce Jamaican sun, Willie had procured a glass-bottomed boat with a canopy. It was moored at the water's edge round the promontory, less than a quarter of a mile from the Frobisher Place. All the microphones were working perfectly, though Toni knew he'd need to go out after dark to renew the batteries on the parabolic. Toni was listening, and recording, when the waiter arrived from the Casa Negra, and gave Sam Bantam a report of the arrival of the guests and the meeting. Sam was less interested in the guests' names than in the date and the time of departure. Veronica continued to wear the locket; Arthur Lovell continued to grumble around the place; Ben went swimming and fishing, and Toni had a few anxious moments when he took his boat near enough to the buoy to see the parabolic microphone, but he appeared to pay it no attention. Samy spent most of his time in bed with one of the girls; the other two had left in the car and Toni heard the rustle of notes as Sam bade them goodbye. 'Give us a ring, anytime,' one of the girls said. 'We're always glad to drop everything and come to one of your parties . . .'

'And drop everything when you get here, eh?' Sam said.

Willie was not married, but his son Absalom was acting as a courier between Toni and Alec at the Casa Negra; so far Alec had not been seen much by the guests, and had stayed in his rooms at the end of the corridor over the restaurant, overlooking the sea. He was sitting in the chair on his balcony when Absalom arrived and handed him a cassette from Toni.

'How do you like your job?' Alec asked him. The boy's smile flashed at him through large, immaculately white teeth, and he nodded his head vigorously. He'd been given a Vespa on which to make his courier runs, and had been promised the Vespa would be his if the job was carried out conscientiously. Nothing could delay him as he dashed down the road past the airport, hoping that another cassette would be waiting for him.

It was. He took it and flashed back down the road.

Three Jamaicans had come to the Frobisher Place by speedboat. Samy had been brought out of bed, and his girl had been dispatched with Veronica to Ocho Rios. They'd been told to book into the Palatinate Hotel and wait until they heard from Sam Bantam. Again Toni heard the rustle of money. The batteries on the parabolic had not lasted as well as Toni had planned, and he had been unable to pick up the bulk of the conversation Sam had held with the Jamaicans on the beach. He had heard enough, however, to know they were to go to the airport and, whatever was their task, they would perform it there. Toni suspected from something he'd heard that they were from Kingston airport. Alec smiled as he listened to the cassette.

The next cassette was a conversation in the house, picked up perfectly by the ice-bucket microphone, which was operated by electrical energy created between itself and the ice bucket, and could transmit more or less indefinitely. He'd had anxious moments when the servant had picked up the ice bucket and had taken it away, but from the sounds Toni heard he guessed the servant had merely thrown the water from the ice bucket over the veranda rail, and had brought the bucket back almost immediately. The conversation was between Sam, Arthur, Ben and Samy.

'So who's gonna do the job?' Sam asked.

'I am,' Arthur said, 'then I'll know it's been done right.'

'Don't trust these other two guys, huh?' Sam said.

'I trust nobody,' Arthur said.

'So when do we go?'

'Ten o'clock.'

'That's early?'

'Yes. I want to be in position in good time. It'll take more than two hours to do the job.'

When Alec heard that he guessed the bi-metal would be the target. Two hours and fifteen minutes to take the panel apart, fix the bi-metal the wrong way round, and clip the panel together again. Whoever Arthur was, he knew the Delta inside out. The bi-metal was copper and phosphor bronze, and would be the first to melt if the plane crashed and burned. It looked similar front and back, but an experienced person would easily know which way to install it. Alec had already made a note for the Chief Engineer, following the Nice discovery, that the bi-metals were to be replaced in every Delta, modified so that they could be installed in only one direction.

The man called Samy, the others, Ben and Arthur, were no problem to Alec. He could arrange to have them identified when they tried to leave Jamaica. They could, of course, be carrying false passports, but somehow Alec doubted it. No doubt they'd flown into Kingston and had crossed the island by car. They'd go out again the same way. Or Sam would plan on taking them out on his boat. If so, they all had a shock coming.

The following day the guests at the Casa Negra all spent relaxing, each in his own way. A party went along to Rose Hall and played golf in the comparative cool of the morning; some went by car for a tour of the island. Others sailed off the beach of Doctor's Cove, lazed in the sun, or went cruising off the island. All day long the barman was busy making rum punches, a delicious confection of milk, soda water, bananas, oranges, and rum, all whipped together with ice into a soothing but insidious drink.

A poker game started before lunch, with a French *duc* and English baronet, the man from Boston, and Madonna, who

157

played with one eye on the game and the other on her girls. By the time lunch was announced, Madonna was winning thirty dollars and had held no hand better than a full house. Madonna had the gift, rare among poker players, that can make or break anyone in the long run, of knowing when to play your cards, and when to jack in your hand. After lunch, those still in the hotel retired to their rooms, and peace descended. Even the barman snoozed behind the bar, and the few people brave enough to face the afternoon heat made do with tea or lemonade from the stall overlooking the beach itself.

Alec Haig spent the entire day in his room, most of the time on the telephone.

There were a few cassettes from Absalom to bring, since there seemed to be an agreement out at the Frobisher Place that they wouldn't talk about the job. Toni had changed the batteries on the parabolic microphone during the night, but there was little for him to pick up. No one left the premises. Sam had a telephone call with New York, and his end of the conversation was recorded through the ice-bucket microphone. He may have had other calls from beside his bed but, with Veronica away, no microphone could pick them up.

Late in the afternoon, Absalom brought a tape with a note from Toni. 'I can't understand these,' the note said, 'but somehow I feel they are important.'

The tape contained one telephone call with two people, both in New York, and Sam Bantam. Prior to the call, the tape had recorded voices which came towards the veranda and went away. Toni had switched to the parabolic to record Arthur, Ben, and Samy on the beach. Ben sounded ill, and sat in a deck chair. The others swam in the pool, then messed about at the water's edge. Toni had been flitting backwards and forwards between the beach and the veranda.

Sam took his call on the veranda, next to the ice bucket. Every word of his side of the conversation was crystal clear. Once again, Alec wished they had bugged the telephone instrument itself, to hear both sides.

Sam Bantam's conversation went like this.

'Hi, Stav, how are things with you?'

. . .

'Fine. Tell Rome I'll talk with him later.'

. . .

'Sure. Sure. Post time. Sure. Sure. Tomorrow morning, for sure. Course I'm sure, I'm riding herd, huh? So, stand by like we agreed, huh. You have mine. It's in the bag.'

The conversation with '*Rome*' was quite similar except that it contained one extra phrase that could have been significant.

'I'm not sure you can ever trust a Greek . . .'

That was all. Alec wound the tape back, and then played it through while he copied down each speech verbatim. Many questions. Who was Stav, and who was Rome? *Post-time*. In American parlance, meant the race would start soon, or the event would start soon. The event was going to take place the following morning, and Sam Bantam was *riding herd,* i.e. supervising the arrangements personally. Then Stav and Rome were going to '*stand by as agreed*' – presumably they were going to stand by to do something when the event had occurred. *You have mine.* My what? Probably my authority, my money . . . *It's in the bag.* What's in the bag? Sam Bantam's money? A document?

Alec could have kicked himself. *It's in the bag,* in American,

159

means, it's a sure thing, it's certain. The event that was going to take place in the morning, presumably, was certain.

But who was Stav, and who was Rome? *I'm not sure you can ever trust a Greek.* What *Greeks* were in aviation? Stav sounded like a Greek nick-name. Was there a Greek in aviation with a nick-name that could be Stav? Sam Bantam called Arthur 'Art', so presumably Stav could be a simple diminutive. What were the Greek forenames beginning with Stav? Suddenly, Alec realised who Stav must be, and why.

Rome, apply the same principles. Rome a diminutive of a fuller forename, and nothing to do with the city of Rome in Italy. Rome. Rome. There weren't many forenames that began with Rome. But then Alec remembered one, Romain...

Now he knew who were the two men Sam had telephoned. And now, he guessed, he knew the members of the syndicate.

The syndicate consisted of Sam Bantam, its leader and general inspiration; Stavratis Theodopolous, a Greek who owned the majority of the shares of an aircraft company in Portland, Maine, which had been doing well with its medium-range jet until the Delta had taken all its orders; and Romain Soltati, a French-Italian who'd made his home in São Paolo, Brazil, and who, by deft manœuvring, had become one of the richest men in that flatulent city. It had been said that Soltati had been behind every crooked politician that crisis-torn country had known during the past twenty years. Dictators had come and gone, but Soltati had stayed, his nest feathered with every change of government. For a while Alec was puzzled by Soltati's interest. What could be his game? So far as Alec knew, no Soltati money was in aircraft shares; his entire wealth was said to be in real estate, most of it in New York and Rio and São Paolo. Alec placed a telephone call to Kenneth Severs in the New York Office, and Kenneth Severs enlightened him immediately. 'Who do you think owns all the land around our building on Sixth Avenue?' he asked.

Alec had to confess he didn't know.

'Amarcado Land Company. And who owns Amarcado?'

'Soltati. So if he can crash our company, buy up our New York office for peanuts . . .'

'. . . he can add it to his own land, and make a thousand million dollars development of it. Instecon crashing is worth at least two hundred million dollars to Soltati. No doubt he already had an option to buy our property, if ever the ground landlord is in a position to kick us out. And believe me, we won't get a day's grace if we can't meet his note when it comes up.'

At nine o'clock in the evening, during dinner, the native band began to play. The Instecon girls were evenly divided throughout the room, Madonna had seen to that, and all were looking good in their evening gowns. Soon each one had a partner and was dancing. The atmosphere was that of a country-house party, with none of the usual tensions that lie beneath the surface on such occasions. None of the guests was of the sort to indulge in peccadilloes or holiday romances; the girls had been picked for their physical beauty but also for their intelligence. Each was devoted to Instecon, each a goodwill ambassadress of considerable potency. Despite their doubtless human wishes – and with such a sprinkling of titles and fabulously wealthy men about who could blame them – all had slept alone the previous night. Madonna had seen to that, too, though that part of her task had not been difficult. Only the journalists had seemed inclined to go beyond the limits, used as they were to junkets in which Public Relations people act as pimps, supplying girls in a further attempt to compromise the press into giving them good publicity. Jacques had foreseen the problem, and the press had been taken to dinner in the town, in a night club known for its available hostesses. The press men had been left to choose for themselves. Half an hour after dinner ended, they were back at the Casa Negra. Jacques was surprised to see them, even more surprised when John Casserotto, from whom he'd received a steady diet of antagonistic needling throughout the trip, elected to be spokesman.

'If we want to get laid, we'll do it under our own steam,' he said. 'This is a pretty good party, and we wouldn't want to miss any of it, or do anything to louse it up.'

Jacques was embarrassed. 'Forgive me,' he said, 'and please accept my apologies. I'm ashamed to say I have misjudged all of you.'

John accepted his hand, shook it, and slapped his other arm. 'Just so we all understand each other,' he said. 'I'm sorry if we're a bit rough on you sometimes, but in the classic words of a paid employee . . . we're just doing our jobs, the best way we know how . . . and the readers have a right to know.'

'No comment,' Jacques said, but this time the general laugh was relaxed, and genuine.

When he had 'bought' the press men a drink, Jacques walked along the veranda and climbed the stairs to Alec's room.

Alec was dressed in a pair of black trousers, black socks and sneakers, and a black woollen sweater of thin cashmere. He had a black knitted woollen hat in his hand, ready to pull on his head.

Jacques looked out over the glistening water. 'This must be one of the most idyllic spots in the world,' he said. 'To think I have an estate not thirty miles away, and I haven't seen it this time . . .'

'You will,' Alec said.' I promise you that when this is over,

162

you can invite me, and we'll bring a couple of girls, and have a very relaxing time . . .'

'You're about ready to go?'

'Yes. Absalom just came with the latest tape. They'll be leaving the Frobisher Place in about half an hour. I want to be at the airport when they arrive.'

'You wouldn't let me come with you? Just in case.'

'You've got a job to do here. But I appreciate the offer.'

Jacques gripped his arm. 'Take care, Alec, I wouldn't want anything to happen to you. I need you to sign my expenses voucher. You know the rules. All directors' vouchers must be signed by another director . . .'

Jacques turned and left the room. Alec watched him go.

Now the moment of action had come again, and once again he felt the icy calm his hatreds generated in him. Alec hated men like Sam Bantam, Samy, Arthur and Ben with the loathing of a patriot for a traitor, a religious zealot for a turncoat. He consoled himself that inevitably, ulcers would get them, a coronary attack or, in the case of Soltati, a revolutionary's bullet.

Willie drove him to the airport in silence. Alec had noticed the damage to the side panel of the car, and caught Willie's reproving stare. Willie had wanted his cousin to be given a taxi to Ocho Rios; Alec had reasoned that nothing would be more certain to make him go than the chance to drive Willie's Lincoln Continental, a prince among motor vehicles. The Lincoln turned off the coast road, and up the road that led to the airport, but then it continued, past the airport, turned right up a hill, and without stopping, over the hill towards the Mountain Lodge, a well-known restaurant and night club. Anyone watching the Lincoln would assume that was where it was going.

Alec was no longer in it when it got to the top of the first hill. He rolled out of the back, and Willie pulled the door shut behind him. Alec rolled off the side of the road and into a ditch. As Willie had said, the ditch was dry there, and lined with soft grass.

Alec waited a moment then rose slowly in the hedge. No one was about. He jogged down the side of the hill, keeping near to the hedge. Once a motor bicycle came up the hill but he was on the ground in the ditch before its light could pick him out, wearing his black woollen cap pulled over his face. At the bottom of the hill he turned towards the airport. Soon he came to the barbed wire perimeter, walking along it until he found the cut section.

He climbed through and walked slowly across the stubby grass towards the airport buildings and the hangars.

The Delta was standing out in the open. It would be hot inside, since the plane had been standing all day in the baking sun. He counted five guards, one at each end of the plane, and three patrolling. He glanced at his watch. It read five minutes to ten. He lay down in the grass and waited. His skin crawled when he felt a lizard creep over him, but when he made a small movement the lizard skittered away rapidly. Beyond the plane he could see the lights of the terminal, and beyond the runway extended to the tip of land at the edge of the ocean. Over to the right was the gaggle of small planes, squatting on the grass like clipped ducks pining to fly. One of them belonged to Jacques de Blaie; he kept it for island-hopping when he was in the Caribbean. Yet another cousin of Willie's looked after it for him when he was away, starting the engine every day and keeping it in good trim. The cousin had worked in England for a few years at the airplane's manufacturers, learning about engines of small planes until he'd saved enough money to come home; now he ran a couple of tourist motor boats in Montego Bay, and dreamed of the day he'd have his own tourist airline.

These thoughts passed idly through Alec's brain as he waited for ten o'clock. All his plans were made, all his men hand chosen, and he could now relax. Unless someone foolishly panicked and pulled a gun or a knife.

At ten o'clock the guard changed and was replaced by a two-man guard only. One stationed himself behind the plane, the other in front. From his position about three hundred yards away Alec could see them both quite clearly. Both came from the airport at Ocho Rios. Their employers didn't know it, or they would never have permitted Instecon to employ them as guards, but Willie had told him that both were drug addicts.

Five minutes after they'd been placed on duty, both lit cigarettes. It might have been Alec's imagination, but he felt he could smell the marijuana, clear across the field.

At quarter past ten the dowser came. It had AIRPORT written all across its side, and was driven by a Jamaican, with another in the cab beside him, and a third riding the tank at the back. The dowser stopped at the plane. The guards had walked forward to intercept it, more curious than alarmed.

Alec saw the dowser operator produce a piece of paper, which the guard who'd been near the tail took and scrutinized. Alec had been crawling forward; now he was within a hundred yards of the plane, but hidden in the grass cut short only along the side of the runways. Ants had got into his clothing and he had an unbearable desire to scratch, but managed to restrain himself. He crawled forward until he was within fifty yards, then thirty, and now he was crouched in the last of the fifteen-inch grass, and could go no farther forward without risk of being seen.

The guards were smoking openly, chatting to the dowser driver. Alec could catch snatches of their conversation, but he couldn't understand what they were saying since they talked in patois.

The service steps had been left at the side of the plane; neither guard could see the other side of the dowser, as Alec could, and neither saw the co-driver's seat tilt forward and the figure, doubtless of 'Arthur', swing across to the steps without touching the ground. Arthur climbed rapidly, bending low, then opened the door just sufficiently to squeeze inside the plane. He pulled the door shut behind him.

Alec smiled. Toni had been busy on that plane, and had installed closed circuit infra-red television cameras while the plane was in London. Those hidden cameras covered every inch of the interior. The cameras used the plane's aerial system as a transmitter, and the signal was being picked up in a room placed at their disposal in the airport tower. 'Smile to the cameras, Arthur,' Alec murmured, 'you're on the television.' To Arthur the inside of that plane would seem black, since he could not distinguish the infra-red light; but to those cameras the inside of the plane would be as bright as any film set. In the room in the tower, Giovanni was sitting in comfort in front of a monitor set coupled to a videotape recording machine. As soon as the door opened, he would have started the recording. George Mason was sitting beside Giovanni, ready to note the engineering significance of any move Arthur made.

And Alec was crouched near the plane, in case anything went wrong. So far everything had gone to plan. He hadn't known about the dowser, but had guessed some inconspicuous airport vehicle would serve as a Trojan horse.

Giovanni and George watched while Arthur went through the complicated mechanism to unfasten the panel. It took thirty minutes before he was able to draw it away from the bulkhead. George whistled in admiration. 'You realize that he's working absolutely in the dark, by touch only,' he said to Giovanni.

'He wouldn't dare risk a light.'

'He's a bloody marvellous engineer, but then I always knew he was. Pity he's got that damned awful chip on his shoulder.'

'You know him?'

'Know him? I bloody well trained him. That's one of my lads, Arthur Lovell.'

Working entirely by feel, Arthur stripped out the bi-metal, quickly reversed it and put it back the wrong way round.

'A lot of lads can't do that in full working light,' George growled, his anger enlarged by his recognition of Arthur's skill.

Alec stayed in the grass, squatting beside the plane. The dowser had left after the driver had gone through the pretence of filling the plane's water cylinders. Alec knew they weren't carrying any water in that dowser, and that it had not come from and would not return to the main building. These men were religious political thugs from the slum villages near Kingston, the same breed of men who'd attacked him at the Casa Negra. At some time they'd worked for the Kingston Airport Authority and had learned the procedures and jargon. But professionally, and by inclination, they were vicious killers, available for hire. No doubt the dowser, too, had been brought from Kingston. Who would think to check a water dowser being driven on to an airfield, with AIRPORT written on its side?

Two and a half hours later the Jamaicans returned with the dowser and gave the guards a story of having lost a

167

bunch of keys. The guards helped them look for the keys on the ground beneath the plane, while Arthur slipped out of the plane, down the steps, and into the dowser in five seconds flat, with the guards none the wiser.

An hour later the guards had smoked five cigarettes each and were sitting on the tarmac, their backs propped comfortably against one of the wheels. They were both stoned, in a state of euphoria that would last until they were relieved at five o'clock. They would not have suspected anything if a herd of Indian elephants had charged across the airfield. Alec got up, and slowly walked behind the plane. Neither one showed any signs of having seen him. He walked cautiously forward from the tail of the plane to the foot of the ramp. Still no sign of alarm. He walked up the ramp and into the plane. The guards hadn't looked back.

In the plane he took up a position in line with the panel and turned to look at the concealed camera.

'Okay, George,' he said.

George came out of the terminal on a bicycle, approaching the rear of the plane, and climbing the steps the way Alec had done. 'Was I right?' Alec asked when he saw him.

'You were right. He changed the bi-metal. Reversed it.'

'Nothing else?'

'No, we watched him all the time. That's a damn good little camera; shows up clear as if it was ordinary light. You'll see it on the videotape. And I know who the man is. Arthur Lovell, one of my own engineers, bugger him.'

George had already started and in less than two hours, working with the light of the torch held by Alec, he had taken the panel apart and had reversed the bi-metal strip. He was damned if he'd let Arthur beat him for time. When he had finished, Alec went back to the terminal, and ordered the guards to be changed. The police came out from Montego Bay to take the two pot-smokers.

*   *   *

Samy and Sam Bantam were awake when Arthur returned to the Frobisher Place, dropped off at the gate by the three Jamaicans, who were taking the dowser back to Kingston by the back road. Arthur had told them he'd been planting drugs aboard the plane for export to England. They didn't give a damn what he'd been doing, so long as they got the balance of their money when they arrived in Kingston with the truck. Sam had given them papers, on a stolen AIRPORT letter heading, to prove they were road testing the dowser after an engine repair. The engine repair part was true; they'd borrowed the dowser from the garage which had done it.

'How'd the job go?' Sam asked, anxious. Samy had known by the smug look on Arthur's face that everything had gone all right.

'What d'you think? I'd bungle it? It went like a dream, and there's nothing to show. Half an hour after take-off, whapp, out go the lights, and down goes the last Delta to fly. They'll never find it, and no airline will run the risk of taking another into service.'

'I'd have been happier if it could have come down somewhere they could find it. Somewhere they could prove it wasn't an unavoidable accident. Jesus Christ, the whole idea is to prove the plane failed because of a fault in the design. How will people know the plane wasn't hit by lightning, or something?'

'Because there isn't going to be any lightning. Not at thirty

169

thousand feet for Christ's sake. This way is perfect. It'll be a mystery, the biggest mystery that aviation has ever known. But don't think they're going to let it off the front pages. Just think how much that plane is insured for . . . Just think what the passenger liability alone is going to cost. The insurance underwriters are going to make an investigation the like of which we've never seen. And while that investigation is going on, nobody, but nobody, will take up a Delta. For the simple reason that nobody will insure it.'

'I guess you're right, Arthur,' Sam said grudgingly.

'You start listening to the radio from nine-thirty tomorrow morning, when the air controller lets it be known to the press that he's lost radio contact with that plane . . . Then you'll know I'm right. And then you can pay us the balance of the money, and we'll scarper. You have got the money here, I hope. You promised us cash on the nail.'

'I have your money here. In dollars like you asked. Have you guys figured how you're going to leave the island?'

Samy looked at Arthur. 'We think we should split up,' he said, 'and we wondered if we could borrow your boat. Ben can drive to Kingston and fly out from there. Arthur and I will take your boat, if that's okay by you, and sail due west. I'll drop Arthur at Port-au-Prince in Haiti, and he can take a plane from there, and I'll go on to Puerto Rico, and leave your boat in a yard in San Juan for you.'

'It's a long way to sail on your own . . .'

'I thought I might take a passenger . . .'

'From Ocho Rios . . .'

'Something like that.'

'Fancy Veronica? You can have her. Why not take 'em both. Arthur can enjoy himself as far as Haiti, and you can gang-bang your way to Puerto Rico. Nothing to beat it, lazing on the deck in the sun, having your ass hauled . . .'

170

'That's a deal . . .'

'Help yourself.'

'Where's Ben,' Arthur said, suddenly suspicious.

'He had to go to bed,' Samy said, 'he's got an attack of the tropical trots.'

'Something he ate?' Arthur asked innocently.

'Yes, I imagine so. If he's no better in the morning we'll need to get him a doctor. I'd hate him to die on us . . .'

'So would I,' Arthur said.

'He can't stay here,' Sam said. 'As soon as I hear that plane's down, I'm closing this place, and taking the first plane out for New York. I don't want to be here when the insurance investigators come looking . . . so you'd better plan on getting him out of here.'

'Poor old Ben,' Arthur said, 'I hope it's nothing serious . . .'

*   *   *

Kenneth Severs was woken by the telephone. He picked up the instrument and held it to his ear, switched on the bed head light, and glanced at his twenty-four-hour clock. It said 0400 hrs, New York time. The telephone operator was on the line.

'Is that Mr Kenneth Severs?'

'Yes, Severs here.'

'Hold on, please. I have a call for you from London, England.'

He heard the twitter twitter as the international lines were connected, and the slow, calm masculine voice of the London operator. He glanced at the dial on his clock that showed London time. Ten a.m. After only a few minutes he heard the

171

London operator say, 'I have your call to New York, sir. Go ahead, your party's on the line.' Then the familiar voice of Entwistle, of Entwistle, Peabody, and Clark, Stockbrokers.

'Kenneth?'

'Bert?'

'Sorry to waken you, Kenneth . . .'

'That's okay, Bert. What's on your mind?'

'You're on my mind, Kenneth. The market's just opened, and you're in bad shape.'

'I know that, Bert. What's the asking price over there?'

'There isn't one, Kenneth. I can't find a jobber who'll touch it. Nobody wants it, Kenneth, absolutely nobody, and the jobbers are holding so much they're scared to death.'

Now Kenneth was wide awake. A *jobber* is a wholesaler, a *stockbroker* is a retailer. The jobber buys as cheaply as he can, then tries to get the best price to sell; he has no contact with the man or the institution buying the shares. The jobber, like any other wholesaler, holds large quantities but if he can't find a buyer he tends to cut his losses and get out. The only way a jobber gets out is to lower his asking price, and this depresses the market price of a share.

'How long will they hold, Bert?'

'It's hard to tell. Already they're walking about with long faces. I think I've heard every old saying that's ever been used on the 'change this morning, and they're all talking about you. Unless they find a buyer soon, I don't reckon they'll hold much longer. And once one of them drops his price it'll fall to the ground. Without a buyer around.'

'Okay, Bert,' Kenneth said, 'I'll take an option on three hundred thousand, but spread it around . . .'

'That's a lot of money, Kenneth, and I'm already carrying you as far as I dare go . . .'

172

'Sure it's a lot of money, Bert. Do you think I'm not good for it?'

'You *are* rather over-extended if you don't mind me saying so. Don't forget you've a settlement to meet the day after tomorrow.'

'I'm not forgetting, Bert. I've already deposited funds with Morgan for that; you should have my note round later today. Look, Bert, let me ask you a straight question. Will you carry me this three hundred thousand, for a short time . . .?'

'How short, Kenneth?'

'Twenty-four hours . . .'

'A lot can happen in that time.'

'If you're in there buying, gently, gently, bit at a time, spreading it around among the jobbers, that should hold the price.'

'They'll know it's private money if we mess about with *options.*'

'Then don't. Look here, Bert, we've got to stop talking round in circles. Let me give you a firm instruction. Buy *at best,* 300,000 shares of Instecon International. No *options,* no nothing, just buy the shares, and debit my account.'

'There's nothing left in your account, Kenneth, that's what I've been trying to tell you . . .'

Now Kenneth's voice was dangerously quiet, calm as the sea before a storm. 'We've done a lot of business together, you and me, Bert, and you've never questioned the state of my account before. If you'd like me to take my business elsewhere, please tell me so . . .'

Bert Entwistle gulped; Kenneth heard him over the telephone and permitted himself a dry smile. The Instecon official business, and the transactions which Bert Entwistle carried out privately for each of the directors, must net him forty thousand pounds a year, tax paid. Plus opening many important doors to him in the City of London, since he was known to have the private ear of the members of the Instecon Board.

'All right, Kenneth,' he said. 'I'll do the best I can. But let me at least exercise my prerogative as a stockbroker advising a client. The way the market looks this morning, here in London, by tomorrow morning at this time those shares won't be worth three hundred thousand pence, and you'll have thrown good money after bad.'

✳   ✳   ✳

Samy and Arthur were sitting in their bedroom, away from all the microphones, from Sam Bantam, and Ben. Arthur was damned proud of himself. 'This is two watch faces,' he explained to Samy, 'and I've glued 'em together round the rim. Now we have a plastic bubble shaped like an oyster, right?'

'Right.'

'Take an ordinary match, break it in half, and glue one end of one half to the centre of the face of one side of the oyster, like this.' As Arthur explained, he fitted his actions to the words. Samy watched him, entranced.

'Glue the other side of the oyster to the inside of this tin of health salts. We'll have to wait a moment for this glue to harden, but it won't be long. Meanwhile, we bodge two holes in the side of the tin, and we take these two hairgrips. Ordinary hairgrips. We wrap this end of one of the hairgrips in plastic, like this, and we stick it through the hole, and we bend the end so that the hairgrip rests on the end of the match.

174

Okay. Yes, the glue's hardened nicely. Now, I wrap this torch bulb in my hanky, and I smash it.' There was a crunch as he tapped with a knife handle and when he unfolded the broken glass he carefully extracted the lamp filament and broke it away from its supports. 'Now we wrap the filament round the end of this second hairgrip, we insulate the middle with plastic, bend it, and place it in the other hole in the health-salts tin and we fiddle about with it like this until it's resting against the end of the first hairgrip, with the filament the only point of contact. He fiddled about inside the tin, his hands as delicate as those of a brain surgeon, bending the springy hairgrip in such a way that the filament made contact, but it was not strained by the pressure. Then he held the two hairgrips apart, took a square half inch of polythene he'd previously cut from a bag, and gently inserted it between one of the hairgrips and the filament. 'You with me so far?' he asked.

'Yes. The match is touching one hairgrip, and the springiness of the grips is holding them together.'

'That's right. Now I connect a battery across the other ends of the hairgrips. The batteries in this torch of course, but I've made these two little holes in the casing so that I can touch each terminal with the ends of these two hairgrips. Just to be on the safe side, I wind these elastic bands round the torch and the health-salts tin, to keep 'em together.'

When he had clipped the two elastic bands round, he picked up another plastic bag, full of powder. 'This is the powder from a hundred smokeless shotgun cartridges. I broke 'em open and threw away the pellets. It's also mixed with the detonating powder . . .'

'I'm damned glad I wasn't there when you prised the cartridges open,' Samy said. 'What the hell are you doing with the powder?'

175

'This,' Arthur said, and slowly poured the powder into the health-salts tin.

'My Christ,' Samy said, 'is that safe?'

Arthur grinned at him. 'Of course it's safe,' he said, as long as that tiny piece of polythene stays next to the filament. Now here's the clever bit. See this zipper case. That's an ordinary toilet case. We open that, and we wipe the lip of the health-salts tin and we put the lid on; we put the tin and the torch into the zipper case; with 'em we put this flat box of shotgun cartridges, and this tube of butane for filling gas lighters. We also put this plastic bag in the case.'

The plastic bag contained a white powder.

'What the hell's that?' Samy asked. 'More explosive?'

'No, that's the health salts I took out of the tin. Finally we put in the glass from the broken bulb. There, we pull the zip round, and we've finished.'

The zipper case was about twelve inches by six inches by three inches, the sort of case in which a traveller carries his toilet articles, or his valeting equipment, shoe brush, polishes, clothing brushes.

'Now we're all ready to go,' Arthur said. 'You've got the idea?'

Samy was mystified. He was more of a theoretical engineer than a practical man, could work out stresses and strains, coefficients of expansion, hardnesses of materials.

'You've got me baffled,' he said. 'A zipper case with a butane gas bottle for filling lighters, a tin of health salts, shotgun cartridges, and a pocket torch. And, of course, an explosive device that would go up if a small piece of polythene weren't held between the contacts by the spring in the contacts themselves. So, what's the secret?'

'This bag is designed to be taken up in an aeroplane, isn't it? and then brought down again. It's designed to be put in somebody's suitcase, in the hold, and the hold of an aeroplane isn't pressurized, like the cabin is. So this little fellow's going to be in an area of fluctuating pressures . . .'

'I've got it,' Samy said, 'I've got it. Arthur, you're a bloody genius. It all depends on what you called the oyster, of course. That's a sealed chamber with plastic walls. At ground level the walls are held in by atmospheric pressure. When the oyster is carried up into the atmosphere, in an unpressurized part of the plane of course, the atmospheric pressure is reduced the higher you go, and so the oyster swells outwards, sucked outwards by the drop of pressure outside, and the ground level pressure inside. When the oyster bulges, it pushes that match stalk, which lifts the hairgrip, and allows the plastic insulation to fall away. Now the contact is broken anyway, and the current can't flow. That oyster will stay that shape as long as the plane maintains height. But once the plane comes down, the atmospheric pressure will increase, will gradually close that oyster again, and allow that hairgrip to spring back until it makes contact with the other. But now the bit of polythene has fallen away, since there's nothing to hold it, and this time, the hairgrips really make contact, the filament glows and the explosive from the shotgun goes boom!'

'That's exactly right. And this is what's so clever about it. If ever they should investigate the cause of the crash, if ever they piece together the bits of metal, what are they left with? A passenger who foolishly packed his health salts, shotgun cartridges, and butane lighter fuel in the same case as his torch and a few of his wife's hair clips. They'll assume the butane gas leaked and the torch fired it.

'Arthur, you are a genius,' Samy said.

For the first time since Samy had known him. Arthur actually permitted himself to smile. It took a long time coming, as if the muscles were out of order, but eventually his face cracked and his eyes shone with the unaccustomed praise.

'Whose bag shall we put it in?' he asked. 'The duke's? One of the princes'? That American, you know the one from Boston?'

'The duke's,' Samy said. 'Sam's pet waiter heard him talking at dinner that night. His bag was opened in Customs coming in. Lightning never strikes twice in the same place...'

❋   ❋   ❋

The baronet and the girl were leaning together by the rail. She smelled fresh and sweet despite the dancing they'd done together. He still smelled of Cologne, a strong masculine smell. He was wearing a midnight-blue evening dress jacket, with a collar that looked as if it would purr if you laid your cheek along it. She resisted the temptation to find out. 'What a magnificent evening,' he said, 'and what a pity you want to end it so early. Look at those clouds, so clean, so pure, so soft . . .'

'I must go in, Sir Frederick,' she said. 'We all have a terrible day tomorrow, and you do have to fly all the way back to England, and we'll never meet again, and well, really, I do have to go and get some sleep.'

'Sleep dwell upon thine eyes, peace in thy breast; would I were sleep and peace, so sweet to rest.'

'Did you make that up, Sir Frederick?'

'No, an ancestor of mine, William Shakespeare. Well, if I can't entice you with poetry, what about a cigarette, Imogen?' He took the gold-crested cigarette case from his inside

178

pocket. His voice had dropped an octave when he spoke again; it had the texture of velvet. 'I have these made for me in a little shop in St James's. I think you'll like them.'

She almost took one; almost! Oh my God, what an evening! They'd never believe her when she said she'd eaten with princes, danced with a duke and, in the nicest possible way, had been propositioned by a Sir. 'No,' she said resolutely. Not for nothing had she been campus cheer leader, not for nothing had she majored in psychology, not for nothing had her class voted her the gal most likely to succeed. 'No, Sir Frederick. I must be strong minded.'

'You're durned tootin' you must,' Madonna said, stepping from the shadow of the climbing bush whose leaves and flowers tumbled in such charming disorder over the rail. 'We all have a long day ahead, Imogen, so off you go and get your beauty sleep.' Sir Frederick knew he was beaten. He raised her hand to his lips. 'Good night, Imogen,' he said, 'with the first dream that comes with the first sleep, I run, I run, I am gathered to your heart. A few words from a work called, appropriately enough, I think, "The Shepherdess".' Imogen gulped, then fled.

'And you, Fred,' Madonna said, 'don't forget to leave your bag packed and ready to go outside your room by seven-thirty ack'emma.'

Sir Frederick took Madonna's hand, and brought it to his lips as he had done with Imogen's. Madonna had the grace to blush.

'Very good, sergeant major,' he said, 'parting is such sweet sorrow!'

✳   ✳   ✳

Alec and Jacques were sitting on the patio near the bar. Alec had changed out of his black gear, and was wearing cool linen trousers and a soft cashmere shirt. Jacques had taken off his tie, and had draped his evening dress jacket over the back of the chair. It had been a wonderful party, charming, unsophisticated, gay, noisy, and above all vigorous. 'Who would have thought we'd have had all those elegant and titled gentlemen playing statues on a dance floor, and bobbing their faces in buckets of water for oranges? I remember all those games from my childhood, but then one was tense, one didn't have the self-confidence to make a fool of oneself.' It had been a hilarious party, a reversion to gay carefree days for all of the people present, an escape from the tight, rule-bound world of big business and high finance. 'I'll never forget the duke doing the limbo beneath a pole, with a glass of champagne balanced on his immaculate chest.' Jacques chortled again, happy, relaxed.

'Your thing went all right?' he asked.

'Easy. We watched him all the way. He never knew. And afterwards, we went into the plane and undid the mischief.'

'And the plane's okay?'

'Sound as a bell. When George had finished, we did a pre-flight check, just to make sure. I've got our best man guarding the plane, and Antonio Giovanni watching them watch it, safe inside the tower. The plane's fuelled, watered, powered and ready to go. But we'll check it again, just before take-off. Just in case.'

A light breeze blew across the water towards them as they sat on the edge of the apron patio, over the edge of the sea itself. The moon had come out strongly, high overhead, and the waves rippled and shone like silver lace. The air was heavy with the night scents of oranges and the sweet odour of tree hyacinths and scarlet flowered aphelandra.

180

'It's going to be all right, isn't it?' Jacques asked, his voice anxious. 'You seem to be a bit cast down . . . You're usually so determined, so confident when it comes to the final moments in one of these jobs of yours.'

'It's going to be all right,' Alec said. 'I wouldn't dream of letting that plane take off if I didn't think everything was under control.'

They both heard the soft footfall in the night, both turned towards the darkened interior of the covered-in dining-room. A waiter came out of the darkness towards them. 'Is there anything else you want?' he asked as he drew near their table.

'Nothing, thank you. You can go off duty if you wish to,' Jacques said.

'I'm on duty, sah, all night in de kitchen, in case de guests wanta cuppa tea . . .'

'Good man. Well, we don't need anything out here, but thank you for asking.'

'My privilege, sah,' the waiter said, as he went back towards the kitchen in the dark recess of the dining-room.

When, ten minutes later, Alec and Jacques saw the waiter go along the veranda with a tray on which was a bottle of whisky and a soda squirter, they assumed someone had telephoned to ask for a night-cap.

*   *   *

'I'm real bad, Samy,' Ben said, his voice pain-racked. He was standing in the doorway of the room which Samy was sharing with Arthur, clutching his stomach. His face was deathly white.

'You going to be sick?' Samy asked him.

181

'I want to be, all the time, but I can't. There's nothing left inside me. You've got to get me a doctor.'

'Okay,' Samy said, and jumped out of the bed, 'hang on a minute while I get dressed an I'll take you down to Montego Bay to that hospital on the right. They're bound to have a casualty department and they'll know how to deal with you.'

Arthur got out of bed, and he and Samy dressed hurriedly. Then they half lifted, half carried Ben out towards the garage. They made such a clatter going through the house that they disturbed Sam, who appeared at the door of his room in his pyjamas.

'What's the matter with you guys?' Sam asked.

'Ben. He's really ill. We're going to take him to a doctor.' Samy said out loud, dragging Ben through the door. Arthur stayed behind.

'You crazy or something? We can't have Ben in hospital, maybe delirious or something, blabbing everything he knows . . .'

'We know that,' Arthur said, 'leave him to us. What the eye doesn't see, the heart doesn't grieve about.' He followed Arthur out towards the car. They bundled Ben into the back, and the car started first turn of the switch. Sam had followed them out of the house. 'Just so nobody finds him,' he said.

'Leave it to us, Sam,' Arthur said, as Samy pressed the accelerator and the car drew forward.

They drove for thirty-five minutes up into the hills, travelling southwards. Ben moaned and groaned and tried to be sick on the back seat, but nothing but a thin dribble of bile came from his lips. The boiled ham Samy had fed to him had been rotten and fly-specked, fit only for fishing bait. Salmonella is a vicious poison. It scours the innards and causes intense intestinal pains. A bad case can rapidly prove fatal unless it is treated. But not rapidly enough. They took Ben out of the car by a mountain stream and told him to drink the water which would ease the pain in his stomach. Ben bent his head over the pool, and after twenty-four hours of vomiting was to weak to resist when Arthur held his arms behind his back, and Samy pushed his head under the water. They left his passport. It was his own, made out to Ben Thomas. Then they laid him on the path by the mountain stream, where someone would be sure to find him. The long trail would eventually lead to the insurance investigators, and take the heat off Samy and Arthur. No one had ever seen them together, no one could connect them and whether the plane fell out of the sky or not they would be in the clear. 'We'll get away on that boat of Sam's,' Arthur said, 'as soon as he's paid us.'

'And we'll take the two girls with us.'

'Yes,' Arthur said, 'I just feel like a bit of relaxation. The two tarts will do nicely, very nicely.'

*   *   *

Alec Haig woke quickly after a few hours' sleep, totally relaxed. He showered and dressed, resisted the temptation to take an early morning swim, and Willie drove him to the airport. Alec walked up into the tower. Antonio Giovanni was still there, having watched that infra-red television set all night. His eyes were bleary and his beard had bristled, but he was still very much alert.

'Nothing,' he said, 'absolutely nothing. No one's been near that plane; I'd guarantee it.'

'You'd better get some sleep.'

'I'll be all right for an hour or two. Anyway, after watching all this time, I'd like to see the take-off.'

'Not worried, are you?'

'You'll be aboard the plane, not me. Why should I be worried?'

Alec put his hand on Giovanni's shoulder. There were not many men Alec trusted completely, but Giovanni and Pappayanakis and Willie were among them.

Absalom arrived at the airport shortly afterwards. He had brought another cassette, and a note from Toni. 'Quiet night,' the note said, 'except that Ben became ill, and they took him away to a doctor. I've marked the tape.' Alec thanked Absalom; he still looked fresh and young and eager, still flashed that devastating smile.

'How's the Vespa?' Alec asked, but Absalom was too full of pleasure to reply. Giovanni had a cassette recorder among his equipment; Alec slipped the cassette from Toni into it, wound it to the marked section, and began to play it. The ice-bucket microphone had caught what Arthur had said to Sam. The expression 'what the eye doesn't see the heart doesn't grieve about' had come through loud and clear.

Alec knew damn well they hadn't taken Ben to a doctor. Ben would be out in the undergrowth somewhere, or up on the mountain, or maybe they'd taken him out to sea, and dropped him in shark water. For a moment he thought of ringing the police – he knew the superintendent in Montego Bay well – but then he stopped. This was no time to involve himself with the officialdom of the law, and the chances were a thousand to one that Ben was already dead.

George had arrived, and Professor Baxter, and with them Alec walked across the field to the plane. It towered above them, majestic and awe-inspiring. Alec had seen it a thousand times but still took a pleasure each time he saw it, poised on the ground, ready for take-off, an eager bird. They climbed aboard, and went into the cockpit. 'Shall you check it, Alec, or shall I?' George said.

'I'll do it,' Alec said.

Professor Baxter was already at work, looking into their eyes with his pin-point torch for the first signs of any administered drug, reading their pulse rates, heart-beats, and skin temperature. All were normal. Then they checked the plane. Everything functioned perfectly, of course.

When all the ticks were on all the pages, Alec turned a worried face towards Professor Baxter. 'Everything's perfect,' he said.

'Well, so it should be, if George did his job right last night. Damn it, Alec, we've had all these people working all night, active and guarding, and now you're complaining because it has all worked, because it's perfect.'

'Look at it from Arthur's point of view. Arthur is an Instecon staff man. He knows our procedures backwards. He knows enough to get Charlie Lamport and Ross Compton, he knows enough to take Faolli out of the way in Rome and then dope Willie Smedhurst – and you know how long it took us to discover Willie's pen had been switched. All right. That man comes to Jamaica and messes about with the plane during the night. We watched him through the television. But he didn't watch us unbug the plane, did he? He must know I would run a check on the plane this morning, and he'd know that I'd discover the bi-metal had been changed. Damn it, that's why he drugged Ross and Willie, so they wouldn't find out what had been done. So why, why hasn't he drugged me?'

'Because he didn't know you'd be the one making the check. And he couldn't drug everybody, could he?'

George had been thinking. 'I don't suppose he imagined for a moment that, having kept the plane under guard ever

185

since it arrived here, we would check the plane again this morning. Of course, he knew the pilot would check it before take-off, but the pilot doesn't do the bi-metal test, does he, any more than the pilot of an airline does it once we've handed the plane over to him as being okay?'

Alec didn't like that, but it seemed the best explanation. Arthur must have assumed that no check would be carried out. The plane had arrived okay, had been guarded all the time it had been here, and there was no reason to suppose it wouldn't fly out again. The pilot would go through his exhaustive but routine check, and the plane would take off. And since it wasn't part of the pilot's routine to check the bi-metal, and the bi-metal was the only identifiable malfunction on the plane, or had been until George put it right, there was no reason on this occasion for anyone to be drugged.

They left the plane together. Alec was in a curious mood, sure but not sure, convinced but not convinced. All his logical reasoning told him that what George said was correct. Arthur and Sam Bantam had bugged the plane during the night. They had no reason to suppose a check would be carried out that morning, since the plane had been placed under such obvious guard since the moment of its arrival. They had no way of knowing the plane had been unbugged. The plane was okay and fit to fly, the check had shown that beyond a shadow of a doubt. Nothing had been planted on the plane and nothing could go wrong with the flight.

The departure instructions were quite explicit. The guests had been asked to leave their locked baggage outside their rooms at seven-thirty a.m. and only carry small hand luggage with them.

The bags were collected shortly after seven-thirty and carried to the truck outside the hotel by the waiters and porters. As each bag arrived at the truck, it was checked to ensure it was properly locked. A waiter collected the bag from outside the duke's room and the room next door in which one of the princes had stayed. He carried both bags along the corridor, had turned right by the reception desk into a small room used for storing brooms, vacuum cleaners and floor polishers. Once inside, he took out the key he'd had made during the night in Montego Bay. It was a copy of the key he'd 'borrowed' from the duke's room the previous night, when he took him his night-cap of whisky and soda. The key worked perfectly. He slipped the zipper case Arthur had given him into the suitcase, then closed the suitcase again and locked it, opened the room door and went out. No one saw him.

He handed the bags to the guard on the truck. The guard checked them both under the watching eye of Hank Dawson. Both were locked. In his haste to close the duke's bag, the waiter had not seen that a portion of the duke's pop pyjamas had jammed itself in the side of the bag, and was hanging out.

'Whose bag is that?' Hank asked, pointing to the hanging scrap of material. The guard read the label and told him.

'I must remember to tell the duke, so that he can unlock it and tuck his pyjamas back in,' Hank said, 'we can't have the ducal night-wear on public exhibition . . .'

Unfortunately, in the rush and bustle of preparing for the passenger's departure, he forgot all about it until the duke was on the plane, and his baggage was stored in the hold, with the Customs chalk mark on its side.

*   *   *

Alec was a direct and straightforward man, despite the deviousness of his job. He wanted Sam Bantam. And therefore he had Willie drive him in the Lincoln Continental out to Frobisher's Place. He gave a card to Tobias, and Tobias took it through to his master, without looking at it. Sam had just started his morning swim in the pool. Tobias returned and asked Mr Haig to go through. 'I know the way,' Alec said, and went through the screen corridor at the side of the house. Sam Bantam was trudging through the water in a fierce stroke that had lots of energy but not much skill.

'Alec, great to see ya! Why don't you strip off and come in?' Sam said.

Alec waited on the side of the pool. Finally Sam finished his daily routine of ten lengths, leaped out, and grabbed his bath robe. A towel was folded on a chair by the seat, and Alec picked it up and took it across towards Sam. On the way across he slipped the Webley pistol out of his pocket, and placed it beneath the towel.

Sam held out his hand. With the other hand he was shaking the water out of one ear, his head cocked on one side. He must have imagined he was hearing things, to judge from the surprise with which he greeted Alec's remark.

'I've got a pistol under this towel, Sam, and if you don't do as I tell you I'm going to shoot you.'

'You what? What did you say?'

'I said, and this is the last time I'll say it, "I've got a pistol

188

under this towel, and if you don't do as I tell you, I'll shoot you." Do you understand me?'

'I understand you, okay, but what the hell, is this a gag?'

'No, this isn't a gag, Sam. Now walk round the side of the house and get into my car. As we get into the car you can shout one thing, and one thing only. "I won't be long, Tobias". If you shout anything else, I'll shoot you . . .'

'This had to be a gag, Alec! Just because I dumped a few lousy shares of yours on the market. Just because I wouldn't play ball on that option deal?'

'Okay, so it's a gag. So I'll now start counting, and if by the time I get to three you've not started to walk towards my car, I'll shoot you. In the knee.' They were just two men having a casual conversation, so far as anyone might be watching could tell. Sam put on his pants and a shirt.

'Okay, so it's not a gag. What the hell. You won't get away with it, so let's play ball for a while,' Sam said. He started to walk towards the front of the house, then towards the car. Tobias appeared in the doorway. Sam saw him, looked at Alec.

'I won't be long, Tobias. I'm just going for a short drive with this gentleman.'

'Okay, get in the car,' Alec said, 'front seat.'

Sam got in the front seat of the car next to Willie, and Alec climbed into the back. The car pulled away from the house. As it went down the drive, another car pulled in. Alec winked at the man in the back who was dressed in white duck uniform, with a flat black hat on which was an official-looking badge. Antonio Giovanni winked back at him. In the car with him were two Jamaicans, who could have been policemen. At the end of the drive another car turned in and came towards them. This time Toni was in the back and he also had two 'policemen' with him.

'What in God's name's happening?' Sam asked. 'Look, Alec, old pal, I'm kinda sorry I screwed up on that deal, but if you'll just tell me what it's all about, I'll make it okay with you. We're both grown men, Alec, and there's no need for us to play rough just over a few lousy shares.'

'That few lousy shares, Sam, was two million. Now look to the front.'

Sam did as he was told. He turned and looked through the windscreen. God damn it, this guy Alec Haig must have blown his stack. And all over a few lousy shares. His hand felt for the handle on the inside of the door. 'The first people I see, I'm going out of this car goddam fast,' he resolved.

Alec hit him on the back of his neck with the butt of his revolver. It was a neat, clean, tidy blow, and knocked Sam unconscious immediately. He slumped forward in his seat.

'Pull over,' Alec said, but he had no need. Willie had already braked and placed the car at the side of the road. Alec opened the door of the front passenger seat; Willie opened the glove compartment and took out the box Professor Baxter had given him. From inside the box, Alec took a cotton wool swab, impregnated it with alcohol from a small bottle Professor Baxter had also supplied, and then swabbed Sam's arm before injecting him with the two ccs of liquid from the hypodermic in the box.

'Let's get to the airport,' he said.

Antonio Giovanni took Arthur in the same way, while Arthur was still in bed. Toni took Samy, but had to fire a shot that grazed Samy's foot. When Tobias came running, one of the Jamaicans had a quick word with him in patois, and Tobias went back to the kitchen convinced he'd seen and heard nothing.

They took Arthur, Samy and Sam Bantam aboard the Delta in hampers used normally for carrying linen, and then placed them in the three forward toilet cabinets after Professor Baxter had examined them. 'They be out for an hour,' he said, 'but I'll keep an eye on them.'

'How long can we keep them out?' Alec asked.

'Indefinitely.'

'And how quickly can you waken them?'

'Any time you say. Just give me five minutes for the antidote to work.'

Alec hung three 'out of order' cards on the doors of the toilet cabinets. 'Bad for the company image,' he said, 'but what the hell.' Nevertheless, he asked the forward cabin staff to stand with their backs covering the notices when the passengers came on board.

Then he left the plane and went to the tower. He sent two telegrams, one to Soltati, one to Stavratis Theodopolous. IMPORTANT YOU COME AT ONCE STOP MEET AT LIBERTY BELLE MOORED AT YACHT CLUB STOP TAKE BOAT OUT FISHING AND I WILL JOIN YOU BY SPEEDBOAT STOP DO NOT TRY TO CONTACT ME. He signed the telegrams 'SAM', knew that Soltati and Theodopolous would get the first plane. A meeting on the high seas would satisfy their love of secrecy; they'd go to the boat, start its engines, take it out on the water, and wait to see what happened . . .

*   *   *

The guests had eaten breakfast on the terrace overlooking the ocean. Earlier, some had taken the last opportunity for a swim in the crystal-clear Caribbean water. All were looking pinker than when they arrived and some were well tanned

even in such a short time. In the absence of morning newspapers conversation at the breakfast tables was animated,
though Jacques had obtained, from the Jamaican *Daily
Gleaner,* a teletype of the Wall Street closing prices. Instecon
shares had plunged over thirty points on the day's trading,
but no one was tactless enough to comment on that. Several
said what a pity they had to return to the cold English
weather, but most would be travelling to the sunnier south
shortly after their return. What's the use of money, if you
don't buy sunshine with it . . . .? One of them, a baronet,
went round the tables canvassing opinions. When Jacques
announced it was time to collect the hand luggage, and
depart for the airport, the baronet rose to his feet and made a
brief speech.

'On behalf of us all,' he said, 'I'd like to thank Monsieur
de Blaie and all the staff of Instecon, for giving us such a
wonderful break in our day-to-day routines. I'll be frank,
not one of us knows what this flight is all about. We haven't
been stuffed with goodwill messages, our support for the
Instecon company has not been solicited. But speaking now
for myself I can say that the company appears to know what
it is doing, and has constructed a truly wonderful aircraft.'

There was a chorus of 'hear-hear' that would have glad-
dened Sir Barton's heart, if he could have heard it. At that
moment he was listening to the closing price of Instecon on
the London Stock Exchange, and not liking it one little bit.

The fleet of limousines was waiting outside the hotel, and
the departure to the airport was swift and effortless. When
they arrived they paraded before Customs, who waved them
through without examining any baggage. It was patently
obvious these gentlemen were not smugglers, or hi-
jackers. The Delta had been parked outside the terminal
building, and they chatted gaily as they went aboard. Though

there was plenty of room for everyone, they sat in small groups, continuing *ad hoc* relationships formed the previous evening. Once they were all aboard, the doors were closed and pressurization of the cabin began while the Delta was drawn by tractor away from the building. The tractor left it on the tarmac, and one by one the engines fired. The plane then trundled slowly to the end of the runway, while the stewardess went through the legal 'life jacket' routine. The flight waited a moment for tower clearance, then started its take-off. In what seemed an incredibly short distance, the Delta suddenly swept on a steep arc off the ground. One minute they were screaming along the runway, the next they could look out of the windows and see the ground apparently falling beneath them. It was like going up in an express lift, smooth and painless, with an exhilarating feeling in the pit of one's stomach as the only sign of ascent. The plane banked almost immediately after its westerly take off, then set a climbing course for England. The SEAT BELTS and PLEASE DO NOT SMOKE lights were extinguished, and the stewards walked down the aisle asking the guests if anyone would like coffee, tea, or any other drinks.

The duke was feeling in a holiday mood. 'I'd rather like a glass of champagne, my dear, if you could manage it.'

She could manage it; she returned immediately with an ice bucket containing a bottle of Bollinger. She wrapped a napkin round the cork, and pulled it, and everyone heard the familiar popping sound. In the first ten minutes of the flight, ten bottles of champagne were popped.

Alec was sitting at the front of the plane with Jacques de Blaie and Professor Baxter. George was in the cabin. When George came through, Alec looked at him. 'Good take-off?' he asked, though George knew there must be a hundred other questions that crowded Alec's mind. 'Everything's fine, Alec,' he said, 'everything . . .'

Alec sat back and relaxed. Thank God for that. All his fears had been groundless. If George said 'everything' that meant he'd checked everything. The plane would take them to London.

Barring acts of God, of course.

He stood up casually and looked down the plane. Everyone was, or appeared to be, happy, talking with his or her companion, drinking coffee or champagne, relaxed. He nodded to Professor Baxter and gently beckoned the two stewards to stand beside him. It looked as if they were having a conversation. Behind the screen their bodies formed, Professor Baxter went into each of the toilet cabinets, and one by one injected Sam, Arthur and Samy with an antidote to the drug that was keeping them unconscious. When he came out he sat in his seat quite normally. Alec sat in his next to Jacques de Blaie, and the two stewards moved back, positioning themselves between the cabin and the toilets.

Samy was first out. Alec saw the door being tried tentatively, then it opened a little, then Samy looked out. Samy was dazed. He stepped out into the plane, no doubt thinking himself dreaming, thinking himself on an ordinary proving flight in the aircraft he knew so well. Suddenly he saw the faces of the passengers, recognized Alec Haig, and fell into the aisle in a dead faint. The stewards came instantly forward and lifted him into a seat. There was hardly a break in the conversation in the body of the plane.

Sam Bantam came out next. He obviously knew where he was. He came out of the toilet like a bull, fully alert. He looked round wildly, then, 'God damn you, Alec Haig,' he shouted, and lunged forward at Alec's throat. Two of the stewards grabbed his arms from behind. He was shouting and cursing and now all the plane was taking notice as the two stewards, themselves strong and well-trained men, struggled to hold him. His feet were flailing wildly and he was banging his head backwards and forwards trying to butt them; they dragged his arms up behind him and held him in a lock, screaming and shouting and cursing Alec Haig.

'God damn you all to hell, Alec Haig, you don't know what you're doing, you don't know what you're doing.'

Several of the guests recognized him, had done business with him in the past. The duke himself came rushing forward down the aisle.

'Let that man go, dammit,' he said. 'That's Mr Bantam, Sam Bantam, I know him personally. Let him go, I'll vouch for him.' The press men realized that this was the start of the story and they were struggling to push through the throng of guests who had risen to their feet and were crowding the aisle.

Alec turned to the duke. 'Please sit down, your Grace,' he said, 'nobody's going to get hurt. Please sit down.' He looked at Jacques and Jacques pushed past him into the aisle, blocking the duke, reinforcing Alec's request that they all sit down. Now Sam Bantam had managed to drag the two stewards half-way down to the floor, but was screaming a different tune. 'You've got to turn back,' he was shouting, 'you've got to turn back at once and land at Montego Bay.'

Alec looked at the third steward who unclipped the micro-phone for the tannoy system and handed it across the struggling bodies. Alec flipped the button, and called into the microphone. 'Quiet, everybody, quiet please, please . . . will . . . everybody . . . be . . . quiet.' The hubbub in the plane died down. 'And now will everybody sit down.'

The guests moved as close to the front of the plane as they

could; somehow the press men got through and they were sitting in the aisle seats. Now the stewards had quelled Sam Bantam in a body lock and he was squatting on the ground like a frog, his head barely visible. 'Lift him up,' Alec whispered, and the stewards used their arm locks to force Sam Bantam into a more erect position. Professor Baxter had opened the black bag on his knee and had prepared a hypo; Alec shook his head, switched off the microphone before saying, 'keep that out of sight, Professor Baxter. I don't want any accusations afterwards that we drugged him to make him talk.'

He turned and looked down the plane.

'Gentlemen, this is Mr Sam Bantam who is known to some of you. Those who don't know him personally will know of him as an investment counsellor. Mr Bantam has just asked me to turn the plane round, to land it at Montego Bay.'

'You've got to do it, Alec,' Sam whispered faintly. Alec pressed the microphone closer to him, until everyone in the plane could hear. 'You've got to turn the plane round, Alec,' Sam Bantam said, his voice now clearly audible.

'Why?'

'Because the plane is bugged . . .'

'What do you mean, bugged?'

'It's rigged. Alec, I'm telling ya, on my Mother's life, this plane will go down into the drink unless you turn it back and land it. How long we been in the air, for Christ's sake?' His voice rose to a shriek. 'How long we been in the air for Christ's sake?'

'Fifteen minutes,' Alec said.

'This plane's been rigged I tell you, it'll crash in another fifteen minutes.'

The minute he said the word 'crash' the plane exploded into a pandemonium, and this time Alec had to shout for a full half minute before he could be heard. When he had restored quiet, he held the microphone close to his lips. 'Listen to me, gentlemen. We must question Mr Bantam, and we can't do it if we can't hear him.'

He held the microphone close to Sam's face. 'Okay, Sam, make it quick, tell me how the plane's bugged, tell me who bugged it and why, and we'll go down into Bermuda.'

'I don't know the technicalities,' Sam said, his voice a pleading whisper which the microphone amplified quite clearly into everybody's ears. 'All I know is the plane will develop a fault thirty minutes after take-off, we'll lose electrics, and the plane will go down. And there's nothing that can be done about it.'

'Who did it, Sam?'

'For Christ's sake, what does it matter who did it?'

'*Who did it, Sam?*'

'A guy called Arthur Lovell. One of your own Instecon guys, from your head plant . . .'

'Who asked him to do it?'

'Will you turn the goddamned plane around?'

'Who asked him to do it . . .?'

'Okay, damn you, I did.'

'You and who else, Sam?'

Sam shouted. '*Turn the plane around.*'

'You and who else, Sam?'

Everyone was listening. Why didn't Alec Haig order the plane turned around? Surely he could interrogate this man Bantam down on the ground?

'Okay, Sam, I'll tell you the names. You and Soltati and Theodopolous; you've formed a syndicate. What were you trying to do . . .'

'Go to hell.'

'Tell me, Sam, tell me!'

Sam stood up straight, shrugged his shoulders. The stewards let him go, but stood ready lest he lunge forward.

'Okay, so I'll tell you. Me, Sam Bantam, and Romain Soltati and Stavratis Theodopolous, we formed a syndicate to try to screw Instecon. We were gonna crash one of your planes. We've already talked your shares down on the market. I hoped to push the shares to the bottom, then pick 'em up cheap. This is a damned good plane. I knew one crash wouldn't ruin you. So now I've made a frank and full confession of my own free will, and I see the press guys have written down every word of it, *for Christ's sake will somebody back there have a bit of sense and persuade this crazy bastard to land this plane!*'

Now the hubbub could not be stilled.

Alec pulled the microphone back and started to chant. 'The plane is not going to crash. The plane is not going to crash. The plane is not going to crash.' It took eight repetitions before the message got through and he had sufficient silence to make his next statement.

'Gentlemen, we knew about this plot. It's true the plane *was* bugged last night by a man called Arthur Lovell. But I personally watched him do it, and afterwards I personally was present when we unbugged the plane. Gentlemen, this plane is perfectly safe.'

On cue, the pilot pushed down his intercom switch overriding Alec's microphone, and when he made his announcement, his voice boomed confidently through the Delta's speakers. 'Ladies and Gentlemen, this is your captain speaking. I've heard every word that has been said and I can verify we are flying at an altitude of thirty-three thousand feet. Nothing is wrong with this plane, and I as the captain am perfectly prepared to go on flying it until we reach London. If a majority of you wishes to do so, however, I will accept your recommendation that we land in Bermuda though I do not see any reason for doing so.'

The duke came forward until he was standing close to Alec.

'This is not some damned silly prank, is it, Haig, cooked up between you and that chap Bantam?'

Alec shook his head. The press were hovering behind the duke. 'What do you think, chap?' he asked.

John Casserotto was jubilant. 'I think this is the best story I've probably ever been given, the best story of my life . . .'

'Do we go down into Bermuda, your Grace?' Alec asked.

'Bermuda? Bermuda? Who the hell wants to go to Bermuda? Can't stand the damned place myself,' the duke said. And that was that. He caught the eye of one of the stewards. 'Now what about a drop more of that champagne, laddie?' he asked, as he pushed through the newsmen and stumped back to his seat.

Sam Bantam was sitting in a seat near the front, his face forward on his chest, slumped in an attitude of absolute dejection.

Jacques collared the newsmen. 'Press conference in two minutes,' he said, 'at the back of the plane, and this time I shan't say no comment.'

The duke came down the plane again with a glass of champagne in his hand. He tapped Alec Haig on the chest with his finger. 'By the way, you bloody young fool,' he said. 'It never occurred to you when you planned your little charade that somebody here might have a weak bladder, and pee himself with fright, did it?'

He pushed past Alec and before he could be stopped he made his way to the second of the three toilets. He pushed open the door. Arthur Lovell was standing there, his face

199

white. 'Sorry, old chap. Didn't know it was occupied,' the duke said, and pushed open the door of the next cabin and went in. Arthur came out of the cabin in a daze, looked at Alec and Jacques uncomprehendingly. 'I'm on the flight,' he said. 'I'm on the flight to London.' And then he started to cackle, an insane sound came from his mouth through the spittle which ran down the side of his chin.

'You knew what I was doing all the time,' he said, 'and you undid it. You knew, all the time.'

'That's right,' Alec said, 'we knew, all the time. We knew, about Ross Compton, Willie Smedhurst, the bi-metal . . .'

Arthur Lovell was chanting the names as Alec said each one. 'Ross Compton and Willie Smedhurst, and the bi-metal, and Charlie Lamport, and Guiseppi Faolli, and the Rome-London flight, and the Montego Bay to London flight, and the bomb in the duke's suitcase, and Ben being killed . . .'

Alec Haig caught the last two items, dragged Arthur Lovell down on the seat where no one could see or hear him. 'The *what* in the duke's suitcase?' he whispered.

'The bomb. I made a bomb. I've put it in the duke's suitcase. Well, I didn't put it in there myself but the waiter, oh, I don't know if you know about the waiter at the Casa Negra, well he was working for us and he put the bomb in the duke's suitcase . . .'

'What kind of bomb? What kind of mechanism? Time?'

'Time bombs tick.'

'Acid capsules don't tick.'

'No, but they're unreliable, aren't they?'

'What kind of bomb have you put in the duke's suit-case...'

And then Arthur told him. After all, a man who knew about acid capsules must have some engineering knowledge and as a fellow technician he would appreciate how clever

200

Arthur had been. Arthur told him about the bomb. And even drew it for him.

The duke's suitcase was in the hold of the plane.

There was no way to get from the plane into the hold without cutting a damned great hole in the floor.

The plane was flying at thirty-three thousand feet and the cabin was pressurized. The hold was not pressurized. If they could cut a hole in the floor of the plane, the minute they penetrated the lower of the three skins, the whole damned plane would explode.

'You say the bomb is armed at this moment,' Alec said.

'It would have armed itself a thousand feet from the ground.'

'And when will it go off?'

'When we descend below ten thousand feet.'

Arthur Lovell seemed to have no more than an engineer's academic interest in the bomb; no sign of fear for his life, no blubbering, 'We're all going to die!' Alec could imagine him sitting there as the plane descended, calculating how high they were, waiting academically for the moment the bomb would explode, turning to say I told you so in a satisfied fashion before the ripping, tearing, blasting force of that bomb blew them all to Kingdom Come.

Jacques had heard the story. Professor Baxter had heard it, and Alec had. To the best of his knowledge, no one else knew it. 'Who else knows about the bomb?' Alec said quietly.

'Only Samy and me, we're the only two . . .'

Alec beckoned to Professor Baxter. 'It'd be a mistake to let Samy wake too soon,' he said. Professor Baxter nodded, slid across to the seat in which they'd placed Samy when he slumped unconscious, and injected his arm. Alec nodded at Sam Bantam, and the Professor went to his seat and injected him, too. Sam Bantam had been in a trauma since his confession; no point in risking what he might become when he realized the new danger in which they found themselves.

'What are we going to do, Alec?' Jacques asked.

'You understand what Arthur was saying?'

'Not all the details, but I realize there's a bomb on board in the hold.'

'That bomb will explode if we take this plane down below ten thousand feet. That means we can't land anywhere. And obviously, we can't fly round for ever. We are carrying enough fuel for five or six hours' flying, and that's all.'

'We can't jump?'

'From ten thousand feet? Even over the ocean, the shock of hitting the water would kill us instantly.'

'And we can't get at the bomb?'

'Not a chance. We're pressurized, and the hold isn't pressurized.' Suddenly an expression came on Alec's face . . . 'Hang on,' he said. 'I may have an idea.' He got up from his seat and walked through to the pilot's cabin. He picked up the headset and clipped it to himself. Then he selected channel 11, private intercom between him and the skipper. 'We've got a bad one,' he said.

'How bad?'

'The worst.'

'A bomb on board?'

'That's right.'

'Then we'd better get into Nassau a bit sharpish?'

'I'm afraid not. It has a negative-pressure detonator on it. Self-arming. It's already live . . .'

'That's a bad one. What's the negative pressure? Give it to me in altitude, save me a calculation.'

'Ten thousand feet.'

The skipper thought for a moment. 'There isn't an airfield that high, is there?'

'Not that I know of.'

'Then it had better be Everest. Look for a glacier?'

'You'd never make it . . .'

'I have enough fuel.'

'I wasn't meaning fuel. I was meaning a landing on a glacier at ten thousand feet.'

'It's all academic, isn't it? I can't go down lower than that, can I, so I have to try. Okay, so I don't make it. Somebody might survive, and we can have choppers hovering over us. They could send out a mountain rescue team ready to pick up anybody who survived. If it's a pressure detonator it must be open-ended and you can guarantee the contacts will touch when we land, they're bound to with that sort of shock. Some of us might survive. And like I said, I have no alternative. I'd better radio Nassau right away and they can get cracking on the mountain rescue side. I'll get 'em to hook me up to somebody who knows Everest, somebody, some-where . . .'

'The Andes is nearer . . .'

'Yes, but there are so many people on Everest these days we're more likely to get somebody on the other end of a radio who can tell me where's the best place to dump it. Might not be a bad landing, all that snow. Anyway, Alec, I'm afraid it's my decision, and that's it. I'm going to dump it down on the most convenient glacier I can find, on Everest, over ten thousand feet.'

'I've got an idea,' Alec said. 'Can I put it to you first? And then make your decision?'

'Sure, I'll listen to any idea at this moment. But once the decision's made, it's made.'

'What's your slowest speed?'

'At what altitude?'

'At twelve thousand feet?'

'Twelve thousand feet, eh? From memory, I'd say it was a hundred and seventy miles an hour. Nearer the ground, of course, it would be slower. There's more air down there to hold us up. In fact, at ground level, we can take this baby down to a hundred and twenty . . .'

'What's the narrowest range of heights at which you can hold?'

'Again, depends what the height is. At ground level I can hold this baby at plus or minus twenty feet, that gives you a forty-foot slice . . .'

'At twelve thousand feet . . .'

'Christ, Alec, up there I'd need a thousand feet . . .'

'Not each side?'

'No, five hundred feet up or down. I could fly her in a flat trajectory, a thousand feet in height.'

'And could you do that at a hundred and seventy miles an hour?'

'Christ, Alec, no. At that speed we'd be going up and down like a yo-yo. I'd need at least a thousand feet each side of me at that speed at that height.'

'But you could do it, with a thousand feet above and below you?'

'Yes, I could. Assuming we don't run into any weather, or any thermals. A thermal right now could drop us two thousand feet without even trying. Or bounce us up two thousand. What are you asking me all this for, Alec, you know this as well as I do?'

'Yes, I'm just checking myself. Believe me, feeling the way I do I don't trust myself an inch.'

'Get yourself a drink and we'll talk some more. Meanwhile I'll get on to Nassau, get 'em cracking.'

'No, hang on, I haven't finished. What height did they fly bombers during the last war without pressurization?'

204

'Ten thousand feet. Any higher than that and you're gasping.'

'Twelve thousand feet?'

'It'd be murder. Look, Alec, if you're thinking what I think you're thinking . . . Certainly we could depressurize the plane. But we have a lot of men back there who are not in the physical condition you and I are in. If you take her down to twelve thousand and depressurize, a lot of our passengers are going to feel pretty sick . . .'

'That's a lot better than dying . . .'

'Who said they won't die?'

'Professor Baxter could check each one of them. Anyone with a dicky heart would show.'

'And then what would you do, Alec? Tell him, sorry, old man, but excuse me while I kill you? You don't have a right to make that decision, Alec. Only I have the right to decide. Do I try my best to get this plane and all its contents on to the ground landing on Everest, God help me? Or do nothing, and circle around until we run out of gas? I'd rather push this rudder away from me right now than hang around for five hours.'

The skipper handed over control of the plane to the co-pilot, came out of his seat, clipped on the headset so they could talk in comfort, away from the responsibility of watching the computer fly the plane. 'Okay, Alec, words of one syllable, and make it quick. What's your idea?'

'Take the plane down to twelve thousand, depressurize the cabin. Use the escape tools to break a hole in the floor through to the hold. I climb down into the hold, and defuse the bomb. From what that lunatic tells me, it'll be simple to pull a wire out of the torch.'

'One thing you're forgetting, Alec. A negative pressure detonator, right? Two points, one pressure controlled. When the pressure gets lower the two points come together. Right? Well, those two points can't be very far apart at this moment, and you don't know where the bag is. What happens if the bag is just beneath where you start using your axe?'

'I never liked that idea in the first place,' Alec said, 'that's why I asked about your slowest speed. Take her down to twelve thousand feet and depressurize. I'll open the door and go out on a harness. The wind force will blow me back level with the plane, and I can open the luggage door into the hold . . .'

'And get your bloody head blown off by a 180-mile-per-hour wind. Do you know racing motorists have snapped their wrists just putting a hand out of the window at that speed?'

'It's worth a try,' Alec said.

It took five valuable minutes but Alec convinced the skipper. It was worth a try, but then, anything was worth a try.

The skipper made the first decision. Should he fly the plane or set the computer to do it? A computer can do the normal detailed things better than any human. It has eyes and hands all over the plane, adjusting here, trimming there, boosting here, retarding there. A jet engine isn't like a piston engine you can feel with your hands, hear with your inner ear. A jet engine needs constant trimming, constant mechanical and calculated supervision. A computer can do that, can quantify the needs of the engine into terms of flow of fuel per second, angle of inclination of rotor blades, pressure of coolant pump, all constantly changing to meet the second-by-second needs of that source of enormous power. The skipper set the computer to fly the plane at exactly twelve thousand feet and one hundred and eighty miles an hour. He trusted himself; but he trusted the computer more.

Jacques informed the passengers what was happening.

He and Alec argued briefly about this. Jacques wanted to hold the passengers at bay on a 'technical faults' excuse, but Alec, sensing the mood, argued 'tell them everything'.

A number of them immediately asked if it was possible to communicate with the ground, but Alec said, 'No'. The press men in particular were furious with him for that decision. 'At least, let one of us dictate the story on a pool basis,' John Casserotto urged, but Alec said no. 'If I'm successful,' he said, 'you can call the story in from London.'

'And if you're not successful?'

'Then who cares?' Alec asked.

He hadn't told them about the Everest plan. The last thing he wanted was an argument at that time. He was busy rigging himself a harness capable of withstanding a pressure of 180 m.p.h., without yanking his arms out of their sockets. Finally he settled for four seat belts. One round each leg, one under each arm pit, and all four tied together in front of his face.

Professor Baxter went round the plane, questioning each passenger about his medical history. Luckily and surprisingly, no one there had a dicky heart, no one had respiratory troubles, no one had asthma. The duke had a weak bladder as the result of a hernia operation, but that didn't count.

Slowly the pressure in the cabin became less and less as the computer matched it to the outside atmosphere while the plane descended. On the advice of Alec, the skipper said nothing to the ground control people except to request, and immediately obtain, permission to leave his flight corridor. The flight control people knew something must be wrong, but didn't interrogate him. However, his position was fixed every half minute, his new course plotted, and a check made on any other aircraft and sea-going craft in his vicinity. Luckily there were no planes at the lower height. Ground control was puzzled when their plot revealed the slow speed at which the Delta was travelling, but again, they did not interrogate the pilot. Privately the tower men speculated the plane had a medical emergency on board, and that the skipper was going down and slowing his speed to make an emergency operation easier. The rule of the sky is quite clear, no interference with the skipper unless he requests it, or endangers his own or other people's lives by his actions; the skipper of the Delta was obviously in full command of his plane and his faculties. Meanwhile the ground controller was in touch with Miami, Shannon, and London, on a purely 'informational' basis.

The plane reached a hundred and eighty miles an hour at almost the same moment as it descended to twelve thousand feet. The pressure difference gauge read zero, equal inside and out.

Professor Baxter made all the passengers cocoon themselves in the blankets the Delta provided and strap themselves into their seats. One press man was allowed to sit erect and watch what was happening. Professor Baxter warned him, 'You'll be frozen silly,' but each had volunteered. Don Berrimore got the job.

The left forward side door was opened. A howling gale immediately filled the plane, and innumerable forgotten objects floated around the inside of the cabin. Four stewards had volunteered to help, and they grabbed what loose things they could, battling their way against the force of gust. One of them crouched down on the floor, forward of the open door, his leg firmly hooked round the iron stanchion. The nylon rope from the lifesaving kit was wound round the stanchion, which was bolted firmly to the floor and to the skin of the plane and normally would carry the emergency chute. Baggage lockers on planes open with a square shafted key. Alec tied the key round his wrist. He was wearing leather-soled shoes which he exchanged for a pair of plimsolls one of the stewards carried for off-duty wear. He borrowed an extra jacket from one of the stewards, but refused any more clothing or gloves since he didn't want to make himself too bulky or clumsy. 'Let's face it,' he said, 'I'm going to be frozen out there, no matter what I wear.' One of the stewards suggested they cut a hole in a blanket, and Alec wear it like a poncho. 'What do I do if it blows over my face?' Alec asked. The three stewards lined up behind the front seats, bracing themselves against the seat backs. Each one was wearing a seat belt, so that should the rope catch him, he couldn't be dragged out of the plane. Alec Haig lay on the floor, his head facing forward, and slowly he eased his feet through the open doorway. The force of the wind blew one of his plimsolls clear of his heel. He snatched his foot back in, and retied the laces so that his shoes could not come off. Then he put his feet out again, pointing towards the back of the plane. The rope was being held by the first man, and Alec felt himself lurch out along the floor under the pull of that knife-edged wind. Already his legs felt as if he'd stepped into an ice-cold swimming bath. Now he was holding on to the side of the doorway, and he circled his body round the lip, slowly letting the wind take him under control. So far the rope had not tightened, and all his weight in that dreadful slipstream was on his hands. And then he straightened his arms; his whole body was now out of the hole and the wind hit the top of his head like an ice-cold sledgehammer. The wind streamed down his hair, past his face like freezing rain; he felt as if his head were drenched, as if ice streams were running down his face and down his collar and around his body. The three stewards took the strain of the rope, and Alec let go with his hands and slipped twelve inches before the rope was taut again and he was lying parallel with the sea twelve thousand feet below and lying on his face apparently on air and looking straight down. He bent his knee, and the force of the pressure against his kneecap almost made him scream with pain, as if he'd put his knee into a running river of sharp sand and the flesh were being scoured from it. His hands were by his side. He dared not lift them. He dared not bend his neck to alter the position of his head and signal to the steward observing him from the doorway, lest the wind pluck out his eyeballs, as he was convinced it would. Somehow he managed to wriggle his body round so that he was lying on his side, and his face was towards the fuselage of the plane, and now the stewards were paying out the line and his face touched the fuselage and without him feeling any pain he saw part of his skin attached to the skin of the fuselage with drying blood on it and he knew that he had stripped his cheek.

For the first time he knew great fear. What if one of his eyes should touch, and the eyeball be yanked out? What if his nose should touch and be torn away? Now the rope had been paid out and he was level with the first aperture and the steward who was measuring his progress against the position of the hatch stopped them paying out more rope and Alec slowly lifted his hand into that searing slipstream and bent his elbow slightly so that his body was held away from the skin of the fuselage and put the key into the hole and turned it. He rapped on the skin of the fuselage with the key, and Professor Baxter, who was inside the plane with his ear glued to the floor heard it. The stewards paid out another three feet of line. Alec moved another three feet backwards and opened another fastener. On the third fastener, the key slipped out of his hand, and would have whirled away like a bullet had it not been tied to his wrist. On the fourth fastener, his hand touched the fuselage and he saw a whole section of his skin pulled away and though he could feel no pain at those temperatures he felt it in his mind and opened his mouth to scream and the whipping knife air smashed into his mouth and he was gasping for breath, almost slammed into unconsciousness by the pressure on his lungs. He held still telling himself, 'I will not go under.' Now the rope was long, and when the stewards let more go so that he could get to the fifth and last fastening, suddenly the rope started to rotate. A spiral of air whipped Alec away from the plane about three feet, spun him round like a crazy top. He tried to push out one of his feet to catch against the plane and stabilize himself but he couldn't move it, so intense was the pressure of the spiral that wrapped him in a corkscrew cocoon. The steward saw this happening, and felt the rope twist in his hands but there was nothing he could do except allow the twist in the rope to snake past him and through the hands of the first steward, then the second steward. If it slipped through the third steward's hands Alec would have been dropped to the extremity of the rope, and the tight twirling must surely have snapped the rope, but as suddenly as it came the twister stopped, and even reversed him sufficiently to brake him. Alec lay there, and slowly let the rope uncurl, sticking out his elbows which banged against the plane each time he came round, but at least kept his face and his hands clear. Finally he was level with the fifth fastening, and this was the tricky one. When the fifth fastening was opened, the door to the luggage hold would drop down on each side of the plane. Two fins, suddenly dropped down, on a plane that was flying near its critical speed, at a critical height. It would be like slapping on the front brakes of a fast-moving bicycle, or at least that was the analogy the skipper had used. Perhaps the doors would not drop down. They were along the length of the plane, so the pressure of wind should not hold them up against the plane, or so they had guessed. Of course, no one had ever opened the luggage doors of a plane in flight before; no one had ever seriously considered what its effect might be. The five fastenings were devised as a safety device; it was quite impossible for those doors to drop open accidentally, so why should anyone consider what the effect would be, or whether they would open or not? Before he put the key into the slot, Alec rapped against the skin of the plane with it. One. Two. Three. Four. Five in rhythm. Then, using the same rhythm, or as near to it as he could keep, he counted to twenty. On the count of twenty he put the key into the slot, still counting, and on the count of twenty-five he turned the key.

The skipper had been counting with him from the moment the professor yelled the rhythm of the taps of the floor over the microphone. When the twenty-fifth tap came, he assumed the plane would suddenly drag. He lifted its nose and boosted the engines. Just a touch. Just enough to cope with the difference in outline . . . Despite the flight corrections he had made, the plane yawed downwards five hundred, seven hundred, a thousand feet. 'Jesus Christ,' the skipper yelled, 'it's going to touch ten thousand!' But it didn't. He had flicked the computer back in the second he'd finished his correction and the computer was fighting every setting, every adjustment to get the plane back to its proper speed and height. The lowest dip was to ten thousand five hundred feet.

Alec was in trouble. The rope had caught around the door flange when it dropped down. Now he could neither move back nor forwards. The rope was jammed between the flange and the skin of the plane. Luckily the door flange was edged with rubber, or it would have sliced through the rope, and the wind would have whipped Alec away. Now he could turn himself on the end of that stump of rope, and the curvature of the door held some of the worst effects of the wind from him. His body was so cold he could no longer feel it. He knew he must be careful. Skiers sometimes become so cold they don't feel the warning jabs of pain when they put their feet in dangerous angles at dangerous places. He knew that he could break a limb easy as pie by putting his weight on it the wrong way, and he would not feel it until the tendons sheered and the use of that limb was denied to him. He dragged his knees towards his chest, and turned his body so that his knees were towards the yawning black hole of the luggage hold. Then he unbent his knees, pushing his feet away from him, at right angles to his body, against the pressure of the slipstream. If he had not been partly protected by the doors he would not have been able to find the strength for this manœuvre, but at last he got his feet inside the hold. A floor ran along the hold supported from the actual bottom by eight-inch aluminium angle brackets. Slowly he pushed his foot around the angle bracket until he could feel his body move forward when he flexed, or thought he flexed, his ankle and knee. This was the dangerous moment. He didn't know if he was forcing that knee against itself, if the pressure he was bringing to bear was actually working against the joint, not with it. Now he reached down with his hands, and could grasp the first angle bracket. He didn't, however. He knew that if he touched it with his bare flesh, he'd strip the flesh from his hand, so cold would the metal be. He pushed his hand through and past the angle, and curled his protected elbow around it. Now, in effect, he was hanging on to the plane with one foot and one arm. He withdrew his foot and slid it along the loading platform where the porters stand to take the baggage off the fork lift truck. Normally that loading platform also would be filled with luggage if the plane had a full load of passengers, but each person on this flight had brought only one bag.

Alec slid his leg along the loading platform, pushing it forward along the plane towards the front. Now he could reach another stanchion, and he wound his arm around that and heaved from his waist and his body slid along the loading platform and at last he was out of the direct force of that searing cutting wind. He lay there for a few moments, gasping for breath in the thin air, reached into his pocket for his handkerchief, wrapped it round his fingers and un-buckled the seat-belt harnesses that had supported him.

The baggage was all stacked forward. He quickly found the duke's suitcase. Thank God he hadn't forgotten to bring the key. He opened the suitcase gingerly, not turning it on its side. The zipper bag was jammed against the pop art pyjamas. As he lifted out the zipper bag, a gust of wind caught the pop art pyjamas, and whirled them from the plane. He started to laugh but didn't move. Then slowly he carried the zipper case to the open door of the plane and dropped it out.

He didn't even bother to watch it go.

He heard the explosion it made at ten thousand feet, saw a brilliant flash of light from astern and below that for a moment illuminated the inside of the luggage hold with a sickly white flare.

He sat down among the bags.

Above his head, he heard the clamour as the passengers and the crew thumped the metal skin of the plane, sending down their praise, gratitude, and relief. The rhythm of the taps came down to him, and almost unconsciously, as in one of those childhood games he spelled out the tune they were banging, and could imagine their voices raised in song.

> *For he's a jolly good fellow,*
> *For he's a jolly good fellow,*
> *For he's a jolly good fellow,*
> *And so say all of us.*

Apart from 'God Save the Queen', it was the only tune the duke knew.

INSTECON

INTERNAL MEMORANDUM Distribution A only

FROM: Head of Accounts

TO: Head of Tech. Sales (Misc.)

My dear Alec,
    I cannot help feeling greater effort
should have been made to trace your White Lady
and recover the Instecon property she must
still be carrying with her. Your report is
vague about her present whereabouts.

See what you can do, there's a good chap.
                        J. C. Crump
                        Head of Accounts

INSTECON
INTERNAL MEMORANDUM Distribution A only
FROM: Head of Tech. Sales (Misc.)
TO: Head of Accounts
Enclosed please find an expense
voucher which I certify as correct.
It related to the recovery of one
locket/pendant/watch, as requested
in your previous memo.

EXPENSE VOUCHER FOR HANK DAWSON:
To travelling to Ochtermochen House,
Aberdeenshire, to procure the return
of Instecon property, as authorized
and instructed. Including taxis,
planes, hire car, tips and gratuities £171.15

To hire from Moss Bros of one
shooting suit, one evening dress for
dining, one morning wear for
attending wedding, plus one shooting
stick, one set of shotguns, one hats,
deerstalker, one hats, top........... £126.15

To hire of one radio receiver to
demonstrate to bride the
inadvisability of taking said
locket/pendant/watch, the property of
Instecon, on her honeymoon with the
Duke of Ochtermochen................. £   4.50

                          Total   £301.80

              Total Swiss Francs   3033.09

Signed Hank Dawson
Countersigned Alec Haig, Head of Tech. Sales
   (Misc.)